THE ROOM UPSTAIRS

A NOVEL

IAIN ROB WRIGHT

ULCERATED PRESS

For Jack and Molly...

"I know a lot of people who've lost their siblings and blame themselves."

Kelsey Grammer

"If a man could have half of his wishes, he would double his troubles."

Benjamin Franklin

"Home is the place where when you go there, you have to finally face the thing in the dark."

Stephen King, IT (1986)

PART I

1

I remember the day it all started, though at the time it seemed like any other Sunday afternoon. The tail end of summer, school was looming ever closer, but I pushed that worry aside as the white-hot sun pierced the centre of an unbroken blue sky and shone down on me. It was 1998, the year of Britney Spears and Furbies. My home was Birmingham, England. I was ten years old, and I was happy.

At that moment, we were all happy.

Except for my big sister, of course. Sarah had been sulking that day, which was no surprise. Since turning fifteen, the entire world had started to irritate her, and doubly so when it involved spending time with our family. That Sunday she had been particularly surly, rolling her eyes and huffing constantly as we ambled between the winding rows of cluttered tables at the local car boot. When I'd been five or six, she had used to let me sleep in her bed, reading to me until I nodded off, but by the time I turned nine she had begun yelling at me if I so much as even dared enter her room. I understand now that it was the indiscriminate virus of teenagerdom, but back then it had hurt me. I missed her.

I miss you, Sarah.

Despite my sister's persistent misery, Mum and Dad were all smiles. They veered left and right across the trampled grass, hand in hand as they perused jumbled piles of clothing, videotapes, and assorted bric-a-brac. I hung back and took my time, enjoying the fresh air and sun. People selling their stuff always excited me, and I loved not knowing what I would find. Ancient things. Strange things. Gross things. I later learned that Australians refer to car boots as *trash 'n' treasures*, and that's exactly how I felt about them. I was Martin Gable, treasure hunter extraordinaire, seeking out invaluable trinkets overlooked by untrained eyes.

Sarah didn't feel the same way, growing even grimmer as the afternoon went on. "I'm bored," she complained, arms folded and a bony hip sticking out as she fanned herself with one hand. The top of a pink thong peeked out from the waistband of her white jeans, which made me feel a little awkward. "Can we go? I want to hang out with Deb."

Dad had his hands in his jean pockets, but he pulled them out and folded his arms. "You can go see Deb later," he said. "It won't kill you to spend an afternoon with us."

"It will if I commit suicide from boredom."

"Don't be so dramatic, Sarah."

Dad and Sarah had always struggled to get along, seeming to get at each other more and more with every passing year. That summer their relationship had been at its worst. He wasn't our real dad, you see – only our stepdad – but as I was only six years old when he'd married Mum, he had pretty much always been 'Dad' to me. To Sarah, though, he was Charlie, the stranger who'd come to live in our house. She had also never seemed to like the fact he was black, which must have hurt him. I doubt she knew quite how much.

That afternoon at the car boot, Sarah had made a sound more insect than human – a throaty hiss – and I wondered if a demon had possessed her, because it would've explained a lot. I also wondered if she would ever be my big sister again, instead of the pimply, thong-wearing devil she'd become.

Don't you ever wish you could go back and appreciate someone more, knowing in hindsight how short your time with them would end up being? I do.

Following Sarah and Dad's brief tiff, Mum tried to play peacemaker. She pointed at one of the tables and spoke in a cheery voice. "Look, Sarah, they have all the *Buffy* videos over there. You love that programme."

"No, I don't. It's stupid."

Mum raised an eyebrow, and I understood her confusion. Sarah had been addicted to *Buffy the Vampire Slayer* only a couple of weeks before. Now she apparently hated it? It was hard to keep track of her personality with how often it changed.

Dad sighed. "What *do* you like then? I'll keep an eye out."

"I don't *want* anything. All this stuff is second-hand. If anyone sees me, they'll think I'm a tramp."

That confused me, and I expressed it. "But if they see you, it would be because they're here, too, so why would they call you a tramp?"

Sarah sneered, probably annoyed that I dared speak to her. "I don't want anybody else's junk, okay? I need new trainers – from a shop."

Mum frowned, then dodged aside as an Asian family barged past with a bag-laden pram. "I already told you, money's tight at the moment, Sarah. I'm sure if you look around you'll find some trainers that are nearly new. No one will know the difference."

"I'll know! No way am I sticking my feet in someone else's shoes. Gross."

I kind of agreed with her there.

"Sarah!" Dad was losing his temper. His fuzzy eyebrows always scrunched up whenever he was mad. "Just stop complaining, will you! If I had the money, I'd buy you a million pairs of trainers, but that ain't life. One day, when you have bills of your own, you'll understand. Money doesn't go as far as you think."

Sarah rolled her eyes. "Then maybe you should get a better job than working in a factory."

Dad's lips pressed together, and he looked away as though he wanted to say something but couldn't. Sarah always made out that working in a factory was a bad thing, but I never understood why. Sure, Dad came home exhausted every evening in filthy overalls, but my friend Mike's dad didn't even have a job. I was proud he was a *welder,* even if I didn't really understand what it was back then.

I'm still proud today.

Seeing Dad upset made Mum angry, and her icy expression made me recoil out of instinct. Even Sarah flinched. "I'm telling you right now, young lady, I have had it up to *here* with your attitude. Keep it up and you'll spend the rest of the summer in your room. Apologise."

Sarah pulled a face. "What?"

"Apologise to your father right this minute."

"He's *not* my father. D'you see an afro on my head?"

I cringed. Dad didn't have an afro – he was bald with a goatee beard – but I knew Sarah's comment had taken things up a notch. My cheeks got hot as I realised people were staring at us, but Mum didn't seem to care. Her icy expression turned into a scowl that was even more terrifying. "Oh, he's not your father? Really? Seems like he's your father whenever you want money or a lift somewhere. How about when—"

Dad interrupted, swiping a palm through the air like he was performing a karate chop. "Let's stop this, okay? I don't know what's happening to this family. All we do is squabble. I hate it."

"I hate it too," I said, still aware that people were looking at us. "It's embarrassing."

Sarah glared at me. "Shut up, idiot."

"*You* shut up. Why d'you have to be so miserable all the time?"

"Because I have to look at you."

I shook my head and turned away. It seemed, more and more lately, that we were mortal enemies, duty-bound to butt heads. I didn't consider the fact I would only ever have one sister, and she clearly didn't value me as her only brother. Maybe if we'd known what lay ahead, things would've been different.

Or maybe they wouldn't have.

Mum was still glaring. "I'm so disappointed in you, Sarah. I never raised you to be this ungrateful."

Sarah's bony shoulders slumped, and she half turned to Dad. "Sorry," she muttered.

Dad put his arm around her and squeezed, but it was awkward because she detested physical contact (another symptom of her turning fifteen). I already missed the feel of her arms around my shoulders while we watched *TV* cuddled up on the living room sofa.

I still miss it decades later.

We walked the rows of tables in silence while I studied various board games that I wouldn't be allowed to buy (they always had pieces missing) and rummaged through a collection of WWF wrestling figures (they were too expensive). I even examined an old picture frame with tiny carvings around the edges. It was pretty cool, but Dad told me to put it down before I broke it. Then Sarah surprised everyone by saying something that wasn't a complaint. "Hey, that's pretty."

She was fondling an old necklace – a dark metal chain with a green glass pendant. The glass seemed to capture the sunlight and hold it, resisting its frantic attempts to free itself. I was no fan of jewellery, but I had to admit it was a beautiful thing in my sister's hand. I still have it to this day, kept safe and close by.

Sarah glanced hopefully at the plump grey-haired woman perched on the open boot of her car behind the table. "How much?" she asked.

"Oh, that old thing? It's ancient – probably an antique."

Sarah huffed. "How much do you want for it?"

"Ten pounds."

Sarah deflated. Car boots were for pocket change, not bank notes. My heart ached a little as her hand lowered towards the table, the necklace hanging from her fingertips. She hated that we were poor, and I guess I hated it too, but it seemed to affect her the most. Truthfully, we could have it worse. We had a roof over our head, a car, and we never wanted for food, but that didn't change the fact that we had to go without things other kids had. The necklace was just one more thing our family couldn't afford.

Dad stepped up behind Sarah and placed his hand under hers. With his other hand, he proffered a crisp ten-pound note across the table. The plump grey-haired woman snatched it away and stuffed it inside a neon green bumbag with PIONEER printed on the front. "Ta, love."

Sarah's eyes glistened. "I-I can have it?"

"Yes, but I don't want to see another frown off you for the rest of the day. Deal?"

"Deal!" Sarah couldn't bring herself to give him a full-on hug, but she pressed herself close and placed a cheek against his chest. For her, it was an uncharacteristic display of affection, and it was enough to make Dad smile. I had never understood why girls loved clothes and jewellery so much. Where was the fun? I would ask myself. Give me a remote-controlled tank any day.

"That was too much," I overheard Mum muttering to Dad. "We're struggling as it is."

"It's fine. The kids should have nice things."

"I don't want you doing any more overtime. We barely spend any time together as it is."

Even at ten years old, I understood that my parents had just made a sacrifice, but I couldn't keep myself from saying what I did next. It was the selfish, age-appropriate behaviour of a ten-year-old, but I still regret it to this day. I imagine most people regret the things they do as children.

"Not fair," I said with my hands on my hips. "I want something too."

Dad turned to me and sighed. "Okay, buddy. Something small though, okay? I know I treated your sister, but I only have a few quid left on me."

I understood I'd won the only victory available, so I nodded and decided a small injustice was better than a big one. A few pounds would do; I just had to make it count.

I got to work, looking at everything – rusty old Matchbox cars and more piece-deprived board games. At one point, I almost gave in to urgency and grabbed an *X-Files* jigsaw puzzle, before remembering that they always had bits missing too. No, I had to be careful about this. I only had one shot.

Sarah glared at me, impatient now she had what she wanted. "Hurry up, Martin."

"I'm looking, I'm looking! I just need to find—"

And there it was... a Karazy Kribs Killer Klown. The films all had 18 certificates, but one night I had stayed up late to watch Channel Four while Sarah was babysitting. She spent the entire night on the phone to her then-current boyfriend, Tom, and so had no idea that I watched the entire film from beginning to end. Sleep had brought nightmares, but after a few days, I stopped being scared and wanted to watch the film all over again. The blood and guts had been awesome.

The Karazy Klown doll slouched on the table was a little frayed, but it was still the sickest thing I'd ever seen. With a bright green mohawk and funky purple lips, it was scary but also silly, which made it just about acceptable as a toy. Was it acceptable *enough* though? "Dad, can I have this?"

"No way, Martin. It's horrible."

"To you, maybe, but Karazy Klowns are the coolest. Mike would die if I had this. It'll teach him for going on and on about the N64 his grandad got him for his birthday." It was a common tactic at that age to use my friends as leverage because they always had more than me. I assumed it made Dad feel guilty, but it probably made him feel ashamed.

Dad glanced at Mum, which was a good sign. It meant he was okay with the doll and wanted to check what she thought about it.

Mum shrugged and looked away, trying to move us along. "It's probably too expensive. Come on."

A scrawny old man behind the table spoke up, his voice

phlegmy, like he needed to cough. He looked ill, but was probably just old. "My grandson's," he explained. "He's off at university and his mother asked me to sell his things from out of the loft. You can have the tatty old thing for a pound, lad."

My eyes lit up. A quid was an acceptable amount of money. "Mum, please?"

She looked at her watch, and it seemed like a good sign – like she was giving up. With a huff, she nodded. "Fine. But if you have nightmares, it's going straight in the bin."

I snatched the Karazy Klown and clutched it against my chest. "I promise, Mum. Thank you, thank you." I looked at the smiling old man behind the table. "And thank you too."

"You're welcome, lad. Enjoy your dolly."

I frowned at that, but it wasn't enough to wipe the smile off my face. It was a very good day.

Or so I'd thought.

2

Because my Karazy Klown had only cost a quid, Dad treated himself to a carved jackal he spotted on the final stall before we made it out to the car park. "I can't believe my luck," he said as he fingered the small wooden animal. He loved to collect African things whenever he saw them because his parents had come from Zimbabwe. It was part of his heritage. Colourful beads decorated the hallway of our house, along with other cool stuff, but my favourite was a wooden spear over the front door (that Mum strictly banned me from playing with). A metalwork giraffe stood beneath our stairs along with various other animal statues, and I imagined that was where the tiny jackal would end up. Sarah always complained about Dad's decorations, saying we lived in Birmingham, not the savannah, but we all ignored her. Sometimes, ignoring Sarah was the only option. At least she was happy now as she placed the green glass necklace against her sun-kissed chest.

It looked old.

Like treasure.

I clutched my Karazy Klown against my chest and

reminded myself I had treasure of my own. Maybe I could dye my dusky blonde hair green to match. Mum would probably have a heart attack, but there was no harm in asking. I could even get a mohawk, I thought.

We headed across the car-packed field and searched for our own. The blazing sun beat at my forehead, and a trickle of sweat rolled down my back. In the distance, the horizon did that shimmery thing, which just proved how hot it was. I hated being too warm, and as much as I loved summer, my favourite time of year was winter. Halloween, Guy Fawkes Day, Christmas and New Year, winter was a leisurely snuggle beneath a blanket with gifts and cool movies. Summer always started fun but seemed to go on too long.

That summer ended up feeling like an eternity.

Mum rummaged in her handbag until she pulled out a sweet that she popped in her mouth. She spoke around it. "Does anyone remember where we parked?"

"Course I do." Dad pointed confidently, but I was unconvinced. None of us had forgotten the day at Merry Hill when it'd taken us two hours to find our car. It was a phobia we all now shared, which made it a relief when I spotted our bright red Vauxhall Cavalier. The fuzzy lion head attached to the aerial confirmed its identity. Despite having spotted it, though, the car still stood a distance away, and the thought of having to walk over to it in the sun suddenly overwhelmed me. I felt the colour drain from my cheeks.

I doubled over and vomited in the grass.

"Ew, gross." Sarah hopped away.

Mum rushed over and placed a hand on my back. The pressure of her palm against my spine was soothing, but it didn't stop me from puking a second time. A taste of metal filled my mouth. Fire filled my throat. Tears welled at the corners of my eyes.

Mum's face creased. She always looked older when she worried, and despite my sickness, oddly, I noticed the greys starting to take root amongst her brown hair. "Honey, are you okay?"

I wiped my mouth and straightened up gingerly. "Y-Yeah, I just… It just came over me."

Dad moved to join us while Sarah stayed back, covering her face in disgust. "Wow, buddy, you're white as a sheet. Maybe you need to get out of this sun."

"He better not puke in the car," said Sarah, "or I swear to God…"

Mum shot her a look, but then her face fell in horror. "Honey, are you okay?"

I turned to see what was wrong, and it shocked me to see blood all over my sister's lower face. "Sarah, your nose is leaking."

Sarah frowned and put the back of her hand under her nose. Bright red blood spilled down her wrist. Then panic set in. "Oh God, oh God."

"Sarah, keep still." Mum dove into her handbag and produced a ball of scrunched-up tissues, which she quickly held to Sarah's face. Within seconds it had turned into a sodden red clump. "Jesus, it won't stop."

Dad looked around frantically. I did the same. Seeing all this blood created another wave of nausea that I didn't want to crash against the walls of my fragile stomach.

There was a lot of blood.

And I was no good when it came to blood. For instance, I had embarrassed myself at school once when Mr Morgan asked me to put out the indoor football nets. A rusty corner had sliced my palm, and I spent the best part of an hour hyperventilating in the nurse's office. Mike still gypped me about it sometimes.

"I'll go get someone," said Dad. I wanted to go with him, but he rushed away before I could follow. Mum had Sarah's blood all over her hands.

I started heaving.

"Not now, Martin. I can't deal with you both."

"S-Sorry, Mum!" I heaved again as a rope wound its way around my guts and someone yanked it up through my throat. I thought maybe I was dying. I definitely could have been dying. My mind filled with newspaper headlines about the tragedy of my youthful end, and I pictured my mum weeping over my coffin. I imagined Sarah laughing.

Dad returned a minute later, clutching napkins in both hands that he must have grabbed from one of the burger or doughnut vans. He dispensed bundle after bundle into Mum's waiting hands, but it took several more minutes before the blood stopped flowing, and by then a pile of bloody napkins littered the ground at my sister's feet. Passers-by seeking their cars grimaced and muttered in disgust. Sarah started to cry, and I knew it was from embarrassment.

"Sarah," I said, "it's okay. It's stopped."

In a rare moment, she looked at me and smiled, albeit weakly. Then she buried her head in Mum's arms and sobbed. Nosebleeds weren't usually a big deal, but there had been so much blood.

So much.

"Let's get ourselves home," said Dad. "Maybe we're all coming down with something."

In agreement, we walked in silence to the car, Sarah leaning against my mum and me clutching my dodgy stomach. I felt better, but a coppery taste lingered on my tastebuds and sandpaper lined my throat. I was thirsty, too, and as soon as I got home I was going to shove my head under the tap and take a long swig. Mum would tell me off for bad manners, but I didn't care. I was that parched.

Dad unlocked the car once we reached it, and Sarah slid in the back without a word. I watched her sympathetically. As much as we fought, it bothered me to see her upset. "Sorry about your nose," I said.

She pulled her seatbelt down and over her lap. "It's fine. How's your stomach?"

I fastened my own seatbelt and shrugged. "I feel okay now. It's weird."

"You really spewed your guts up. It was gross."

Her attitude was gradually returning, so I decided to disengage. I turned and leant against the window, welcoming the cold glass against my clammy forehead. Mum and Dad hopped into the front seats and made the car bounce, which my stomach didn't appreciate.

I took deep breaths.

Don't be sick in the car. Don't be sick in the car.

Don't think about all the blood.

"Buckle up," said Dad, even though we'd already done so, and he slid the key into the ignition. When the engine came to life, it sounded wrong – like a robot coughing.

Or laughing.

The disturbing sound went on for several seconds until Dad threw himself back in his seat and punched the steering wheel. "*Machende!*"

Machende was an African word Dad used whenever he got mad. Mum stared at him. "What is it?"

"It won't start. Must be the battery." He punched the steering wheel again. "This is turning out to be a horrible day."

Sarah and I groaned in chorus. We didn't know it then, but the horrible days had only just begun.

3

Dad solved the Sunday afternoon crisis by asking a man with a BMW to use his car phone. We waited an hour until an oil-covered old man charged our battery with some leads that looked like crocodile mouths. He then gave Dad a piece of yellow paper that made him groan. Once we were all set to go, Dad started the car in silence, showing no pleasure in it being fixed. At home, he called around local garages to find a new battery as cheaply as possible, but from the look on his face, he failed to find a bargain.

A few days passed, and thankfully none of us got ill. My stomach remained settled and Sarah's nose didn't bleed. That didn't mean things were normal though. Six bulbs in our house blew on a single day, and the chunky microwave Mum had saved up for stopped working. Two dead pigeons ended up on our garden table, rotting in the sun. The last thing to happen was the TV in our lounge turning slightly purple – just enough to be annoying. Dad's mood grew increasingly bad as he fretted about all the things that were going to cost us money we didn't have. The atmosphere in the house turned tense. I couldn't relax, and my bladder complained constantly. I kept needing to take pathetic little wees, like the frightened beagle puppy my friend Mike had once looked after for a family friend.

Things didn't *feel* right.

In fact, they felt wrong.

It was eight o'clock on a Friday evening towards the end of August when I found out just how wrong things were. I remember it being a Friday because of the wrestling. They called it *Monday Night Raw*, but that must have been American timing or something because it was always on at the end of the week. For me, back then, Friday was wrestling night, filled with the likes of D-Generation X and Stone Cold Steve Austin. It was on late, but Dad was doing overtime and Mum had gone next door to share a bottle of wine with Diane, our next-door neighbour. She often did that whenever Dad worked late, and if she stayed home without him, she got sad. I wondered if she missed him or if it was something else.

What else could it be though?

Sarah was babysitting, but as usual she paid me no attention. She had a boyfriend in her room with her named Courtney, which I thought was a girly name, but other than that he was okay. When he'd arrived that evening, he'd given me half a pack of *Rolos* from his pocket, which automatically made him nicer than most of Sarah's other previous boyfriends (and there had been many). Mum had a rule about keeping bedroom doors open with members of the opposite sex, but like with most rules, Sarah ignored it. I could grass on her, of course, but it would be more trouble than it was worth. I was happy enough watching my wrestling without having to worry about my sister shagging some guy with a girl's name.

I settled down on my bed in front of the small television I had got on my last birthday and switched to the satellite channel. I needed to watch whatever was playing down-stairs as Dad had snaked an aerial from the Sky box in the lounge out through the wall and up into my room. Because the lounge was empty, I could watch whatever I liked, and I had already set it to the sports channel, which was one of our family's rare extravagances (Dad couldn't live without the cricket or boxing).

The Undertaker was in the ring tonight, threatening to bury Stone Cold Steve Austin alive and take his belt. Under-taker was my favourite, but Stone Cold was cool too. In fact, I'd been thinking about asking Mum to let me shave my head like him. Surely I wasn't far from growing a beard either, now that my eleventh birthday was less than a month away. I pictured myself as *Stone Cold Martin Gable* and grinned.

A glass of fizzy apple juice was perched on my chipped bedside cabinet along with a chicken sandwich I had put together myself – a Friday night ritual because Dad always did the shopping that day. Fresh chicken and fizzy pop is one of the fondest memories of my childhood.

I grabbed the drink and took a big swig, anticipating the sweet bubbles that would erupt inside my mouth...

... then spat it back into the glass. "Ew! Flat? What the hell?"

The bottle of pop had been unopened – I'd broken the seal myself when I'd taken it from the fridge – yet it tasted like rusty water. Where were the bubbles? The sweetness?

To get the taste out of my mouth, I grabbed the chicken sandwich and took a big bite. I choked. The rancid meat fell from my mouth and I gagged into my hand. The grey, half-chewed mass made me groan. The slices had been a healthy, delicious white when I'd placed them between the bread. How the hell had it spoiled so quickly?

Something wasn't right.

I tipped the chewed mess from my palm onto the plate and grimaced. Knowing my parents, they'd probably bought a load of expired junk from the supermarket's bargain bin – it wouldn't be the first time. I'd taken quite a liking to stale doughnuts and funny-tasting yoghurts.

I looked up at my Karazy Klown doll, which I'd proudly placed on the shelf above my television. It seemed to stare back at me, grinning with its swollen purple lips. My tummy rumbled and I felt I needed to explain. "Man, I'm starving. I wish I had a big fat Big Mac. It's been months since I ate a McDonalds."

The doll continued staring back at me and I swear I detected pity on its face.

My bedroom light flickered.

The television blinked out. Stone Cold disappeared mid-swear word. For a moment, I thought there'd been a power cut, but then the lights stopped flickering and stayed on. I lay on my bed, breathing in that tense air that seemed to blanket the house lately, and glanced back at my Karazy Klown.

It moved.

No way, I thought, and I pulled my legs up the bed away from the shelf. Bug eyes fixated on me, the doll leant forward until it fell off the shelf and thudded on the floor. I yelped, but then I laughed. It wasn't alive, just unbalanced.

The TV blinked back to life.

I yelped again.

There was a knock at the door and I yelped a third time. "What the hell?"

My overeager bladder kicked in and I suddenly needed

to wee. It wasn't until a second knock at the door sounded that I realised someone was lurking outside on the landing. I glanced over at my Aston Villa clock – almost nine. Mum shouldn't have been back for another hour.

"Yeah? Who is it?"

"Who d'you think, Sonic the Hedgehog? It's Sarah."

I hopped off my bed and approached the door. I opened it carefully, suspicious of what she might want from me at this time of night. My nose detected something unusual.

Something wonderful.

Sarah clutched a small cardboard box with flashes of red and yellow. She thrust it at me, holding it right underneath my nose. "Courtney went to get us a Maccies but I only fancied a few fries. I was gonna chuck it in the bin, but he said I should give it to you. It's a Big Mac."

My eyes widened and I automatically reached for the cardboard box. My fingers clamped around the corners, but I kept my eyes fixed on Sarah, fearful she might yank it away and laugh.

"Don't worry, I didn't gob in it. Courtney's mate works behind the counter so he didn't even have to pay. Still, you better say thanks when you see him."

"I will." Courtney had just gone up in my books, so saying thanks wouldn't be difficult. This was exactly what I had wanted. Screw chicken sandwiches for tea.

Sarah waved a hand dismissively. "Go on then, idiot, and don't tell Mum about me shutting my door."

"I won't." I closed the door and hopped excitedly onto my bed. I placed the Big Mac on my lap and opened the carton slowly, half expecting Sarah to have placed a rock inside – but no, it was real.

It smelled real.

I lifted it with both hands and took a massive bite.

It tasted real.

Heaven.

Somehow, an unexpected McDonalds was even better than one you knew was coming – like a gift from God. I chewed slowly, savouring every mouthful, and as I did so my eyes scanned the room, settling on my fallen Karazy Klown. The doll lay on its side, bug eyes staring at me. I swallowed the food in my mouth but didn't take another bite because something had occurred to me.

I had wished for a Big Mac.

4

Despite my reservations, I devoured the rest of my Big Mac like a hungry vulture, and yet I averted my eyes from my Karazy Klown the entire time. Mum always told me I had an overactive imagination. That was why I'd been terrified of water for an entire year after watching *Jaws*. The problem was, I was both curious and sensitive – two things that didn't mesh well. "You ask questions and get disturbed by the answers," Dad would always tell me. But knowing about myself made it easier to cope, and that was why I knew I was being silly by thinking my Karazy Klown had got me a Big Mac. It was ridiculous. Of course the doll hadn't got me a Big Mac.

I decided to take my plate downstairs and get a glass of water – seeing as the pop was flat – and then I would settle down to watch my wrestling as planned. Before I left, though, I replaced my Karazy Klown on the shelf, and this time I pushed it further back to avoid it falling off again. Then I headed downstairs.

As predicted, the tiny wooden jackal Dad had bought at the car boot sale had joined the animal collection in our hall. It now perched on the floorboards between a stone elephant and a plastic flamingo. A pair of wooden giraffes towered on both sides. A few more animals and it would make quite the collection. Strangely, the jackal was facing the opposite direction to the other animals. I couldn't resist bending down and turning it to face the same imaginary horizon as the elephant and flamingo, but as I balanced the plate of spoiled chicken sandwiches in my one hand and rotated the statue with the fingers of my other hand, I felt a pinch.

"Damn." I put my thumb in my mouth and sucked it. It didn't hurt too badly, but I could feel a wooden shard beneath my skin. "Stupid splinter."

"You all right, dude?"

I jumped, bashing my ankle against the radiator on the wall behind me and almost dropping the plate of sandwiches. When I saw it was Sarah's boyfriend, I resisted crying out in pain, not wanting to embarrass myself in front of another boy. To go with his girly name, Courtney had floppy blonde hair, but he seemed pretty tough otherwise. Sarah had a massive crush on David Beckham and had clearly got herself a cheap copy. "Oh, h-hey, Courtney. I got a splinter, but it's nothing."

"Shit, I hate that. One time, I was playing roller hockey and I got one off my stick the size of a nail. Hurt like a motherfucker for days. I use an aluminium CCM now that's much better."

I chuckled, impressed by the casual swearing. Dad had zero tolerance for bad language, and even Sarah rarely dared cross that line, so Courtney was playing a dangerous game by swearing in our house. Seeing as it was just him and me, though, I supposed it was okay. "Yeah, I um, shitting hate splinters."

Courtney grinned. "How was the Big Mac, dude?"

I blushed. This older lad had indirectly bought me dinner, which was weird. I didn't know why, but it was.

"Yeah, good, thanks. I was starving."

Courtney tapped me on the shoulder. "No probs, little man. Your sister sent me down to grab some CDs. You know where they are?"

I nodded. Sarah scattered her CDs all over the place, alternating between her Walkman, the big stereo in the lounge, and the small one in her bedroom. I didn't mind most of what she played, but when Mum and Dad were out, she pushed her luck with the volume. "I'll show you where they are," I told Courtney, "but can you tell her to keep it down? I'm trying to watch telly."

"Sure thing, dude. I'll make sure it's not too loud."

I smiled, unused to being listened to when it came to Sarah. "Most of her CDs are in the lounge, I think."

Courtney followed me while I led him to a pile of CDs on the coffee table. He tried to pick them up with one hand, failed, and then carried them in both. He thanked me, then said, "So, what you watching?"

"Huh? Oh, um, just, you know... wrestling."

"Sweet."

"Really? Sarah says it's all stupid and fake."

"You can't fake being dropped on your head by a seven-foot monster in a mask, can you? I reckon it's all real."

I beamed. Part of me knew wrestling was all a big set-up, but it was fun to pretend. "Okay, well, I'll catch you later, um, dude."

Courtney gave me a wink and headed back upstairs. I went into the kitchen with my plate, shoving the chicken sandwiches and the Big Mac carton into our dent-covered pedal bin. The stench was terrible, and I wondered how I hadn't noticed before.

Curious, I decided to check out the rest of the slices in the fridge – the fizzy apple juice also warranted closer inspection. Maybe if we returned the items to the supermarket we could get a refund. Money was too tight to waste on spoiled food and drink, right?

The door on our fridge always stuck, which meant you had to plant your feet nice and firmly on the lino before giving it a hefty yank. I did this now, but the door was stuck even tighter than usual. It took several yanks, and the gritting of my teeth, to finally pull it open.

The stench slapped me in the face and I immediately started gagging. Flies erupted from the fridge in a buzzing black cloud. I yowled in disgust, but at the same time my sister began blasting *Backstreet Boys* at full volume and drowned me out.

Thanks for nothing, Courtney.

I stared into the fridge and saw rotten food on the top three shelves. The eggs in the side door had turned black and green. The chicken slices were covered in fuzz. Vomit erupted in my throat and I had to turn, spattering the linoleum with chunks of Big Mac. My vision tilted and I stumbled out of the kitchen, back into the hallway. I had to place my hand to my mouth as more vomit spilled out. With tears in my eyes and my stomach in knots, I scrambled to the stairs on my hands and knees. I tried to call out, but my throat was clogged.

What was wrong with me?

I made it onto the landing. Sarah's room was on my right, just past the bathroom, and I clambered towards it, fighting the urge to vomit again. Once my stomach was marginally under control, I then did something unthinkable – I barged into my sister's room without knocking.

What I saw next is vaguely imprinted on my mind even now, years later, but at the time it had been a disorientating blur. Sarah and Courtney were lying on her bed. Courtney was topless and Sarah was in her bra and a pair of silk shorts. Her brown hair was a tousled mess. I think my mind shut out most of the other details, but I do remember that green glass necklace sitting against her bare chest. I also remember how furious she was with me – and how much I didn't care.

"Martin, you little brat! Get out of my room."

Courtney leapt up and pointed a finger at me. "Not cool, dude. I thought you were all right."

I ignored their outrage. "Th-The fridge. You have to come see the fridge."

Sarah started putting on her T-shirt. Once it was over her head, she glared at me. "What are you talking about, you idiot?"

"Just... please, come."

Courtney wasn't as friendly as he'd been downstairs, and I didn't like the way he scowled at me, so I backed up towards the door, keeping my eyes on Sarah. Maybe she sensed the horror on my face, or perhaps it was curiosity, but she sighed and shook her head. "Fine, I'll come look. Stay here, Courtney."

Courtney looked put out, but my sister whispered something to him that made him calm down. He sat on the bed and told us to hurry.

Sarah followed me downstairs, huffing irritably the entire time. I remained silent. The only way to explain what had rattled me so much was to show her. Our fridge was a disease pit when only an hour ago it had been normal. As a ten-year-old kid, I didn't understand how that was possible, but Sarah was nearly an adult. She'd know what to do, right?

We had to clean the fridge.

We couldn't just leave it.

Stepping into the kitchen, Sarah spoke up. "What do you want to show me? It best not be anything gross."

"Just open the fridge, but hold your breath first."

She frowned, and I wondered if she anticipated some kind of trick, like I had when she'd given me the Big Mac. This was no joke though, and I was glad when she gripped the fridge handle and yanked. I turned my head and shielded my nose. Held my breath.

"What is this, Martin? What the hell?"

"You see? Do you see it?"

"See what?"

Huh? I turned my head to look inside the fridge and once again the stench hit me. More flies escaped and buzzed around the kitchen. "C-Can't you smell that? Can't you *see* that?"

Sarah turned and glared at me as if she'd never met anyone so stupid. But she was the stupid one. Didn't she recognise rotting food when she saw it?

I pointed a finger at the fuzzy chicken. "It's gone off. It's disgusting."

"What are you talking about, idiot?" She reached inside and grabbed the packet of chicken slices. I grimaced at the mere fact she could touch it, but when she peeled back the plastic – unleashing an extra putrid odour – I had to cover my mouth to keep from throwing up again. My burning throat could take no more abuse, but Sarah sickened me further by pulling out a slice and sniffing it.

"Sarah, it's rotten. Put it down!"

She rolled her eyes and did the most horrifying thing I could imagine. She fingered the slice of slimy chicken into her mouth and chewed.

That was too much. I rushed over to the sink and heaved my guts up, but my stomach was empty. All I could do was retch and moan.

"What the hell is wrong with you?" Sarah demanded. "Do I need to fetch Mum?"

I wiped drool from my mouth with the back of my hand and groaned into the sink. "Sarah, why are you messing with me? Just tell me you see the mouldy food."

"I don't see anything. The chicken tasted fine."

I pushed against the counter and turned myself around. Sarah continued glaring at me like I was an idiot, which caused anger to take hold as I decided this was beyond cruel. "You're a liar, Sarah. It must have tasted like... like... oh no!"

Sarah shrugged. "Like what? Why are you looking at me like that?"

"Your nose is bleeding again."

Sarah put the back of her hand against her nose and once again saw blood pouring down her wrist. She didn't panic this time, however, having dealt with the same situation less than a week ago. It was becoming a regular occurrence.

Was she ill?

"Move aside," she said, barging her way to the sink. I was about to protest, but then my eyes caught sight of something that shocked me – something that made me wonder if I was going crazy. The fridge was clean. The food inside was normal. The flies had gone. "I-I don't believe it."

I bent over and vomited over the floor. My stomach hadn't been empty after all.

5

D espite her bleeding nose, Sarah had enough pity to help me. She grabbed a tea towel from the cupboard and placed it against her face to catch the blood, then placed her other hand on my back while I retched, rubbing firmly but gently. Sweat dripped from my every pore, summoning a chill as it soaked my clothing.

"You're burning up, Martin. I need to get Mum."

"N-No, don't leave me. Please."

"Then let's at least get you in bed."

I agreed and let her guide me out of the kitchen. Her nose was still bleeding, which caused her to bump into the walls, half-blind, but she didn't take her hand off my back the whole time. We reached the stairs, and once again I clambered up them on my hands and knees. This time I moved like a snail and Sarah had to keep pushing me.

We encountered Courtney on the landing. He had put his T-shirt back on and no longer seemed aggravated. In fact, he looked freaked out at the state of us – my sister bleeding behind a tea towel and me covered in bile and chunks of Big Mac.

Sarah growled. "Move out the way, Courtney. Martin's ill."

"What's wrong with him?"

I groaned. "I'm sick."

"No shit." Courtney rushed to my bedroom door and held the door open for us like a doctor awaiting a patient. "Take deep breaths, little man. You'll be all right."

"I'm not a little man."

"Okay, fine. Take deep breaths, big man."

I didn't know if he was trying to be funny or not, so I ignored him. Leaning against the wall, I dragged myself through the doorway and into my room. It felt like free falling as I flopped towards the bed, and my legs almost collapsed before I made it there. It was a relief when I crashed down on the mattress.

Sarah leant over my bed, her necklace catching the light and shining in my face. It hurt my eyes and made me groan. "We need to strip you off," she said. "You're too hot."

I looked across at Courtney, concerned about him being there while my sister tore off my clothes, but he'd turned to face the wall. Once more, I liked him. I knew I had ruined his night, but he wasn't holding it against me. He was trying to help.

My stomach began to settle, but my head throbbed. Once my clothes were off, my body cooled, but not by enough. I rubbed my legs against the frigid sheet, trying to cast off more heat.

"He was fine ten minutes ago," said Courtney. "And what's with your nose?"

"I don't know," said Sarah. "It just started suddenly, like it did last weekend."

"You had a nosebleed last weekend too?"

"Yeah. Martin was sick like this too."

"Weird."

"Yeah."

My head pulsed with agony and my sister's glittering necklace still hurt my eyes. "The light. Turn off the light."

Courtney stood closest, so he reached over and hit the switch. My TV was still on, but its muted glow was bearable. In the darkness, it made my room flash and strobe, which added to my nausea. Sarah started touching my forehead. I batted her away. "Stop. Stop touching me."

"Here, drink this." A glass touched my lips and instinctively I took a sip. My mouth filled with sweetness – fizzy apple.

"It tastes right. It tastes right."

"What are you talking about, Martin?"

I shoved my sister away and sat up in my bed. My vision blurred, but I managed to look at her. "Sarah, I swear to you, everything in the fridge was rotten. I swear."

"Martin, you're ill. I think you have a fever."

I couldn't hold myself up, so I flopped back onto my pillow. Courtney appeared, holding something out to Sarah – a cold, wet flannel that she placed on my forehead. After the initial shock, it was amazing. My panicking gradually stopped. I lay still.

Then the house shuddered.

The front door slammed.

I heard the *clink* of Mum throwing her keys down on the hallway's sideboard.

Thank God. I need you, Mum.

I tried to speak, but Sarah shushed me. "I'll go get her," she said.

While Sarah hurried downstairs, Courtney sat on my bed. "You'll be okay, dude. Just a tummy bug."

"I'm sorry."

He frowned. "What for?"

"Messing up your night."

He punched me gently on the leg. "Don't worry about it. What was the deal with the fridge though? What happened in the kitchen?"

I managed to sit up again. "I made a sandwich and it was... it was rotten. I checked the fridge and there were flies and maggots and..." I could see he wasn't believing me. His eyebrows rose and he looked amused. "Never mind."

"Just hallucinations and shit, ain't it? I remember when I got tonsillitis about your age. Thought the Teenage Mutant Ninja Turtles were tryin' to eat me."

I laughed, and covered my mouth when I accidentally spat in Courtney's direction.

"Hey, don't infect me with your AIDS, dude."

"Sorry."

"You apologise too much."

Mum came barging into my room and headed for my bed. She looked worried, but also bleary-eyed. "Honey, what's wrong?"

"Little man was sick," said Courtney.

Mum looked at him and exhaled. "Thank you, Courtney, but it's late. I assumed you would've already gone home by now."

"Oh, um, yeah, I was on my way out but then Martin got sick so I stayed to help. I'll go now, Mrs Gable. Sorry." Courtney had pale skin, but his cheeks turned a shade of red now. The way Mum had just spoken to him was mean considering he'd been looking after me.

I had to speak in Courtney's defence. I usually hated Sarah's boyfriends – Dillon had punched me in the back – but I liked this one. "I wanted him to stay, Mum."

Courtney gave me a small nod that I thought meant

thank you. Mum softened a little. "Okay, well, thank you for helping, Courtney, but I don't want you getting in trouble. Sarah will see you tomorrow, okay?"

Courtney gave a small bow. "Happy to help, Mrs Gable. Hope you feel better, Martin."

I waved a hand and let it flop onto the bed. I felt a brief throb that reminded me of my splinter. Courtney headed out of my room and I heard him go downstairs. Minutes later, the front door slammed again.

"Let's turn off that racket," said Mum, turning the knob on my TV. From the looks of it, Triple H and Shawn Michaels had been about to close the show, letting loose with a bunch of groin chops. Where had the time gone? My Aston Villa clock said it was approaching ten o'clock.

Mum put her hand against my forehead. Her lips were bright red as she gave me a thin smile. "You're still hot. Let me get you some paracetamol."

I pulled a face because I hated having to swallow pills. I would always gag and choke, certain I had something stuck in my throat for hours afterwards. When I was three, I apparently choked on a sausage and nearly died. Although I didn't remember it, it must have disturbed me enough for me to still have a problem with swallowing. And sausages.

Mum shuffled out of my room, leaving me with Sarah. Her nose had finally stopped bleeding, but dry gore now caked her face. She looked like my Karazy Klown's girlfriend. "Mum's had a skinful," she said quietly, and she didn't seem happy.

I shrugged. Mum got tipsy with Diane once or twice a week, and sometimes more, but I didn't see why it bothered Sarah so much. I changed the subject. "Your nose has stopped bleeding."

"Yeah. Hopefully Courtney can get the image of me

covered in blood out of his mind or he'll probably dump me."

"He won't. He seems nice."

Sarah smiled but then frowned. It clearly dawned on her that we were being friendly instead of arguing, and as I was no longer ill her obligation to be nice had ended. "Yeah, well, thanks for screwing things up tonight. He must think we're a right bunch of weirdos."

Mum returned and Sarah used it as an excuse to leave. I propped myself up against the headboard and took the pills Mum offered on her palm. "Drink this," she said, handing me a glass of milk. "Might settle your tummy."

I took the glass and moved to pop the pills into my mouth – but I paused.

Mum put her hand against my forehead again. "What is it, honey?"

"I don't feel ill any more. My stomach is... okay."

"Well, these things sometimes come in waves."

"Yeah, like at the car boot. It came and went just as suddenly then. Mum, what's wrong with me?"

Mum blinked sleepily. She looked old again, which meant she was worried. "It's just a tummy bug, honey. Take the pills and try to get some sleep, okay?"

I didn't feel like sleeping. In fact, I was upset I'd lost the evening to sickness. The wrestling had finished, and it was too late to do anything else. "Can I stay up for half an hour, Mum? I'm wide awake."

Mum smiled. It was always easier to get my way when she'd had a drink. "Tomorrow's Saturday, so you can watch TV for a while longer. Nothing scary though, okay?"

"I promise."

Sarah shouted from the landing. "Mum! I need you!"

Mum groaned and turned around. "What is it now, Sarah?"

"You have to come see this. Right now. Seriously, hurry. Oh my God."

I sat up in bed. A bad feeling came over me, and this time it wasn't nausea.

6

Sarah's voice had sounded odd. Not worried or annoyed, just... *flat*. Shocked, maybe? Her room was further along the landing than mine, so I couldn't see her or Mum as I sat alone on my bed. Something wasn't right, and my head conjured images of a masked killer dispatching my family. I had to stop myself from getting carried away. "Mum, what is it? What does Sarah want?"

She called back to me. "I... It's... There's a..."

Something was definitely wrong.

No longer feeling ill, and instead full of dread, I leapt out of bed and hurried across my room in my boxer shorts. I found Mum and Sarah on the landing, staring at something ahead. They presented an obstacle to my short frame, so I had to shoulder them aside to get a look at whatever had captured their attention. At first I saw nothing out of the ordinary – just the carpet and doors – but then I realised what was out of place. "I don't understand."

Sarah looked at me, eyes so wide it looked like she didn't have eyelids. "You see it, right?"

I nodded. "A door. There's a door there."

"Please tell me you kids have something to do with this," said Mum. "Did you call Jeremy Beadle to come and play a prank on me? Where are the cameras?"

I stared at the strange doorway on our landing – strange because it'd never been there in the ten years I'd lived there. It looked just like the others – four panels and a brass handle – but it was also completely alien. It didn't belong here. "Mum, I swear I had nothing to do with this."

"Or me," said Sarah. Her face was still coated in blood, and her horrified expression made her look like a ghoul. "I mean it. This is well weird."

I agreed wholeheartedly. How could a door just appear on our landing with no explanation? It made no sense.

We shared that wall with our neighbour, Diane, but I doubted she had anything to do with this. She was an alcoholic according to Sarah, and only left the house to scrounge money off the neighbours to buy sherry. Diane was always nice to me, though, and Mum had known her for years. She didn't strike me as someone who could secretly build a doorway between our landings.

I stepped a little closer to Mum, my surprise giving way to fear. "I don't like this, Mum. How did it get here?"

"I have no idea, Martin. I think... I think maybe there's been a gas leak and we're hallucinating. We should get out of here."

It was the same thing I'd thought earlier when I'd found the spoiled food. Gas made you all light-headed and crazy, right? I'd seen it on an episode of *Casualty*. Sarah was shaking her head though. "If we're hallucinating," she said, "how can we all be seeing the same thing? How is that possible?"

Mum was silent for a moment, then clapped her hands together. "Okay, kids, we're getting out of here."

Sarah started laughing. It was a crazy laugh like a villain in a cartoon. It was a sound I'd never heard her make before. "I wish Courtney was still here. This would blow his mind."

Mum put a hand on each of our shoulders and pushed us towards the stairs. My body was buzzing, tiny bugs racing through my veins. Terror and confusion. I was also strangely amused by the ridiculousness of it all.

Why am I afraid of a door? I asked myself. Because it shouldn't be there, was my simple answer.

We made it downstairs and hurried for the front door. Mum grabbed her keys off the side table and turned them in the lock, but when she opened the door she leapt back and screamed. Sarah and I screamed too.

Courtney flinched on the doorstep and did a little dance. He clutched his chest and sucked in air. "Shit, you scared me to death, Mrs Gable. What are you all doing at the door?"

My mum recovered from her fright and grabbed hold of her anger. "What are you doing back here, Courtney? It's late."

He took a step back, forced to retreat by my mother's furious glare. "I-I forgot my house key, and I didn't want to ring the bell because my dad's got a shift early in the morning."

"You must have left your keys in my room," said Sarah, "but we're leaving."

"What d'you mean, you're leaving? It's eleven o'clock at night."

"Babe, it's impossible to explain. I wish you'd been here earlier."

I jolted. A heavy feeling spread through my chest like I was drowning in custard "That's the second time you've wished that, Sarah."

She pulled a face at me. "What?"

"Upstairs, you wished that Courtney was here. Now he is."

"Yeah, so? What's your point, idiot?"

I shrugged. "Just saying."

But what was I saying? That something made my sister's wish come true? Like mine had when I wanted a Big Mac?

Don't be stupid, Martin. Don't get carried away.

I tugged at my mum's arm. "I want to get out of here."

"I know, honey. We're leaving right now."

Courtney held up a hand. "Wait! I need to get my keys first. Unless it's okay for me to stay here tonight and—"

"You're not spending the night with, Sarah," said Mum snippily. "If you need your keys, be my guest and go upstairs to get them. I suggest you do it quickly though."

"No," said Sarah. "You can't go up there, Courtney. It might be dangerous."

Courtney frowned. "Dangerous? What the hell is going on?"

"Nothing, I just don't want you to go upstairs, okay?"

"Okay." Courtney barged past us into the hallway and paused at the bottom of the stairs. He peered towards the landing, then turned to look back at us. "I'm going to get my keys, so why don't you just tell me what I'm going to find up there?"

We all looked at each other. How could we explain about the strange door without him laughing in our faces?

I found my voice before Mum or Sarah did. "We thought we smelled gas. Just be quick because we need to leave."

Courtney looked at me suspiciously, then started up the stairs. "Wait for me, okay?"

Sarah hugged herself nervously. "We will, babe, I promise."

"You have less than one minute," said Mum.

I watched Courtney stomp up the stairs, wondering if we had done the wrong thing. What if something happened to him up there?

Like he gets eaten by a door.

Insane.

We waited silently in the hallway, the front door hanging open behind us and letting in the summer night breeze. I was still only wearing boxer shorts, which caused me to shiver. It would be humiliating if anyone saw me, yet the thought of dashing back upstairs to find some clothes was terrifying. That strange door might open up and spill monsters onto the landing. As much as I wanted to be a grown-up, right then I wanted nothing more than to be treated like a child.

A thump sounded from upstairs.

We flinched.

We waited.

Courtney appeared at the top of the stairs and quickly stomped his way down. At the bottom, he held his keys out and jangled them. "Found 'em."

Sarah grabbed him and hugged him. "Didn't you see anything?"

"Huh? What are you on about?"

"Did you see a door?"

Courtney looked left then right, and when he focused back on my sister he had a smirk on his face. "Um, yeah. I used one to get in your room. Seriously, what's going on?"

This was taking too long. "Courtney," I said, "there's a weird door on our landing. Didn't you see it?"

He looked at me like I was mad, and I wondered if that might be the case. I certainly *felt* crazy, and if men in white coats came to take me away, it wouldn't have surprised me.

Courtney put his hands on his hips. "I don't get the joke.

Can you all just be normal, please, because I'm getting confused."

"Babe, there's a door," Sarah blurted out. "Just like Martin said."

Courtney turned to look up the stairs, seemingly irritated rather than afraid. With a grunt, he said, "Enough of this. I don't understand what you're doing, so just pack it in right now."

I was a little taken aback by his tone. Courtney was a year or two older than Sarah – he was learning to drive – but he had just shouted at us all like we were little kids, including my mum. Her face tremored like a firework about to go off, but then she calmed down. "I suppose it's understandable you think we're all mad, Courtney, but something strange is happening that we can't make sense of. That's all you need to know, okay? We're going outside to figure things out."

Courtney continued looking up the stairs. "What did I miss? What's *really* up there?"

Sarah reached out to take his hand. "It doesn't matter, babe. Just come outside."

"No way. I want to know what's happening."

"Nothing is happening. We're just being silly. Please, just come on."

"Someone is up there, aren't they? Did they break in?"

"What? No! Courtney—"

"Okay, that does it." To our horror, Courtney dashed back towards the stairs.

Sarah called after him – "Don't go up there. Please!" – but he ignored her, so she ended up racing after him.

Mum tried to grab her but missed. "Sarah, get back here right now. Sarah!"

Sarah disappeared up the stairs, calling after her boyfriend the entire way.

I looked at Mum, wondering what we should do. "I want to go outside."

"We can't without your sister."

"Mum, I'm scared."

She laughed, but I didn't like the sound. "There's nothing to be afraid of, sweetheart. It's just a door."

"But where did it come from?"

"I... I'm sure there's a reasonable explanation." She cupped her hands around her mouth and yelled. "Sarah, come back down here at once. Sarah!"

No reply – at first – but then: "Mum! Help!"

"For Christ's sake!" Mum bounded up the stairs and suddenly I was alone. I felt the night at my back, the breeze on the nape of my neck. The fear of standing there alone, late at night, by an open door, became too much to bear. I hurried up the stairs. Sarah's voice was all I heard as I approached the landing. She sounded frantic.

"Mum, he went inside. He went inside."

I found Mum and my sister staring at the mysterious door again, but Courtney was nowhere to be seen. Where the hell was he?

"The door opened," said Sarah, her voice wavering like she was about to cry. "He went inside, Mum. He went inside."

I could see Mum's hands shaking by her sides. She clenched them into fists and yelled at the mysterious door. "Courtney, I demand you come back out here at once. Courtney?"

Courtney gave no reply. The door remained closed.

"Right!" Mum stepped forward, her hands shaking even

more as she reached for the door handle. "Last chance, Courtney."

Still no reply.

Mum cursed under her breath then pushed down on the handle. It moved an inch, but no more. She shoved her shoulder against the wood. The door didn't budge. It didn't even rattle.

"Courtney!" Sarah pulled at her hair, which was still a mess from earlier. "Courtney, are you okay? Say something, for fuck's sake."

Mum shot her a look, letting her know that the bad language had not gone unnoticed, but the situation was too tense to make an issue of it right now. I wondered if I could get away with swearing, then decided it wasn't worth testing. "Are we still going outside?" I asked, wanting to leave now more than ever. My head was a jumble of thoughts. Why the hell did Courtney go inside? What was behind the door?

Mum must have been thinking the same thing. "What happened up here, Sarah?" she demanded. "What on earth made him go inside?"

Sarah shook her head, tears in her eyes and clotted blood staining her face. "He said he saw something. Then he just ran in. The door closed right after him."

"D-Did you see anything?" I asked, my voice tinny and childlike.

She scowled like it had nothing to do with me, but then she must have realised I wasn't trying to stick my nose in or make trouble. I was just her scared little brother. "I didn't see anything," she said. "It was completely dark inside. Courtney couldn't have seen anything either."

Mum rattled the handle again, but it still refused to budge. She ended up standing with her hands on her hips and just staring at the door.

"Are we still going outside?" I asked her.

"We can't leave," Sarah snapped. "Not without Courtney."

Mum kicked the door, banged on it with her fists. "God-damn it, Courtney, get out here. Answer me!"

A clicking sound.

The door opened with a menacing *creeeak*. I remember that sound now, years later, with absolute clarity. It was the sound of something mocking us.

Mum stepped back and gasped. She might have turned and run, but I could tell she was forcing herself to stand there and face the room. She was the adult; she couldn't panic. Not if Courtney was in danger. He was in our house, which made him our responsibility.

I wrapped both arms around myself and shuddered. "Mum, what's in there?"

"I don't know, Martin. Be quiet."

Sarah took a step forward. "Courtney?"

Mum let out a breath that turned into a growl. "Okay, enough of this." She shoved the door and pushed it all the way open. The room was unlit, but the light from the landing spilled inside and illuminated the interior. I leaned around my mum to see. Would I see a magical portal? Or a fantastical realm filled with dragons and fairies?

No.

All I saw was an empty, featureless room. The walls were a light colour, possibly white, and the floor was smooth – no wooden boards or carpet. It was the emptiest room I had ever seen.

Sarah bent forward and tried to see inside without having to step closer. "Courtney? Courtney, where are you?"

It made no sense, but Courtney wasn't inside the room. I hadn't seen him go inside, but where else could he have gone? I edged back until I was in line with my bedroom, then nudged the door to look inside. Courtney wasn't there either. "Check the other rooms," I said. "Maybe he's winding us up."

"He's not hiding, you stupid idiot."

Mum pointed a finger. "Sarah, don't talk to your brother like that. I want you to check the other rooms just like he told you; and this best not be a joke or you'll be grounded for life."

Sarah rolled her eyes. "I can't believe this."

Like the stroppy teenager she was, Sarah barged open the door to the bathroom followed by the door to Mum and Dad's room. Courtney was inside neither. The final room was Sarah's own, and she grumbled to herself as she opened the door. Even from where I was standing, I could see that the room was empty. Her boyfriend wasn't hiding inside.

Courtney was gone.

Impossible.

Sarah put a hand to her face and started to sob. "Mum? Mum, where is he?"

I crept towards the stairs. "Mum, I don't like this. Can we go?"

"It's okay, Martin." Mum had lost all the colour in her cheeks and she no longer seemed drunk. "It's okay."

But it wasn't okay.

Sarah's boyfriend had disappeared.

I stared into the blank, featureless room that shouldn't have been there and wondered what it had done with Courtney.

Soon, I would find out.

PART II

7

Thinking back to that night is a strange and difficult thing. Have you ever had a memory that is blurry yet crystal clear at the same time? It doesn't make sense, I know, but nothing about that night does. It was a nightmare come to life, and I still haven't woken from it completely.

I remember Mum ushering us downstairs while Sarah protested. I was so freaked out that I skidded on the hall-way's wooden floorboards and almost fell, and it was only my momentum that kept me upright and hurled me towards the front door.

Which was now shut.

It'd been open when I'd gone upstairs. There was no doubt in my mind.

I grabbed the handle, but it didn't move. Mum's key was still in the lock and I tried to turn it – totally stuck. "It won't open," I cried.

"Move out of the way." Mum eased me aside and tried the key herself, but she gritted her teeth and pulled back her hand, sucking on her thumb as if she'd hurt it. It reminded me of my own thumb, and the splinter I had got from the jackal statue. I looked at it now and saw reddening flesh.

"Damn thing is stuck tighter than a jam jar lid," said Mum, pulling her thumb from her mouth and shaking it irritably.

Sarah slumped against the bannister. "We're locked in?"

"We'll have to try the back door."

And so we did, dashing through the hallway into the kitchen. The back door was old, with gaps in the wooden frame that let in cold air. It was also stiff and heavy, difficult to open. Tonight it turned out to be impossible. The key was jammed just like the one in the front door. The handle wouldn't move.

"Try the phone," said Sarah.

"Good idea," said Mum, grabbing the handset from the wall beside the fridge and dialling a number that I could tell wasn't 999 – too many key presses. I assumed she was calling Dad. After a moment, she tapped the phone against the wall. Then she prodded at the buttons on the handset like she was trying to squash bugs. I didn't like her expression. She was getting worked up.

Someone should've picked up by now.

Sarah wiped tears from her eyes and cut streaks through the blood still caking her face. Her whole body shook. She was terrified.

I felt utterly bizarre – like I had somehow left my body and was watching the whole scene unfold from above. My life until that point had been more or less ordinary. At some point I had changed dads, but I barely remembered the original, and when I was eight I had got chicken pox and needed to stay off school for a week. Finally, when I was nine, I fell out of a tree and twisted my ankle badly enough to need an X-ray (it was fine), but other than those three things, I considered my life boringly normal. Now I suddenly found myself caught up in a real-life episode of the *X-Files*. A room had appeared in our house and it had made my sister's boyfriend disappear.

Had it abducted him?

Could it be aliens?

I laughed and tried to stop myself, but the sound escaped in a clipped guffaw that made both my mum and Sarah glare at me. "Sorry," I said. "I just feel like I'm going to wake up from a nightmare any minute."

Mum pulled me into a hug. Usually, I would've resisted the dramatic display of motherly affection, but it was exactly what I needed. Safety in her arms. Sarah joined us, and the three of us just stood there, hugging for several minutes.

Eventually Mum broke away and went to put the kettle on. "The main thing," she said, "is that we don't panic. We're all okay, aren't we? Let's just have a cup of tea and sit for five minutes while we talk it all through. Does that sound okay?"

I felt very grown-up being consulted like that, so I agreed wholeheartedly. Minutes later, I was sitting in my dad's armchair with a piping hot cup of tea in my hands. At first, nobody said anything. We just sipped our drinks and stared at the threadbare carpet long in need of replacing.

It was Sarah who eventually spoke first. "What if Courtney's hurt?"

"I'm sure he's not," said Mum. "How well do you even know him, Sarah? You can only have been seeing Courtney a couple of weeks because you were with Darren before that."

My sister blushed and looked away. I didn't understand, so I stayed quiet and let the conversation continue without me.

Mum's eyes narrowed while she waited for Sarah to turn

back and face her. "Sarah, how long have you been seeing Courtney?"

She shrugged. "I dunno. Two months, maybe."

"So, while you were seeing Darren then? Classy."

"Me and Darren were never serious, Mum."

"He was heartbroken when you dumped him. I suppose that was so you could be with Courtney?"

Sarah shrugged again. "I could have carried on going out with both of them, couldn't I? I dumped Darren as soon as I knew it was serious with Courtney. Anyway, who are you to talk, Mum?"

Mum's face turned sour, and I waited for her to lash out, but she didn't. She just sucked in her lip and chewed on it for a moment. Eventually, she asked a question. "So, it's serious?"

"Yeah, so what?"

"Well, he seems like a nice lad, I suppose. A little old, perhaps."

Sarah rolled her eyes. "God, Mum, he's seventeen. All my friends go out with older lads. The boys in my year are all dickheads."

"Language, Sarah."

I rolled my mug back and forth in my hands, spreading the warmth through my fingers. "Courtney's all right. I like him."

Sarah gave me a brief smile, but no verbal reply. Maybe she was happy that I liked her boyfriend, but it must have annoyed her too. Anything I liked was, by default, childish and uncool.

"It would be a shame," said Mum, "if Courtney has anything to do with all of this... strangeness."

"He doesn't, Mum," Sarah almost shouted it, "so will you

just stop with that? He went into that room and disappeared. Is that so hard to understand?"

"Yes, actually. Do you kids have any idea what's going on? Any playground talk you can share that might make sense of this?"

I frowned. "You mean like ghost stories or something?"

She looked at me and shrugged. "I'd take anything right now."

When it came to playground ghost stories, I had a ton, but one came immediately to mind. "I heard the local tip is haunted. One night, ten years ago, a girl named Annie May played hide and seek with her friends. She hid inside a fridge and couldn't get out again. When the workmen arrived in the morning, they threw the fridge in the crusher and pressed her flat as a pancake while she was still alive. Her bones and all the metal fused together. They never found the body, but if you visit the tip at night, you might see her. Annie May will smile at you and you won't be able to breathe."

Mum grimaced. "Why are you telling me this particular story?"

I shrugged. "I think it's cool."

"It's rubbish," said Sarah. "Everyone knows the story of Annie May. It's made up."

"No, it isn't. Mike told me his big brother went to school with her."

"Well, Mike's a liar. Kids have been telling that story for years. Anyway, how do you know she was crushed in a fridge if no one ever found her body?"

I opened my mouth but couldn't find an answer. She had made a good point.

Sarah rolled her eyes. "Idiot."

Mum put her mug down on the coffee table with a clink.

"Sarah, will you stop? Getting at your brother isn't helping; and Martin, while I appreciate your story, it doesn't help our situation, does it? Don't you have anything relating directly to what's going on?"

Sarah put her head in her hands. "This is so stupid. We should try the doors again. They stick. We just need to pull them harder."

"They stick in the daytime," said Mum, "not late at night. Besides, it hasn't even been that hot today."

"Still, I think we should try the doors again. We need to get help for Courtney."

Mum nodded. "I know, honey. Let me get things straight first though. So, Courtney went into the room and the door closed behind him? Did he close it?"

Sarah shook her head. "It was more like a gust of wind blew it closed. He yelled something to me, but as soon as the door closed I couldn't hear a thing. Mum, I'm worried about him."

"Try to focus on what we're doing right now. So we'll try the doors again. And if they're still locked?"

"We try the phone," said Sarah.

"And if it still doesn't ring out?"

"We wait for Dad to get home," I suggested, staring into the last of my tea. It had gone cold remarkably quickly.

Mum glanced at her watch. "Dad won't be home until gone three. You kids should be fast asleep by then."

I scoffed. "You expect us to go to bed?"

"I don't know. Maybe. Okay, so I'll go and try the doors again. Sarah, can you try the phone to call Dad, please?"

Sarah put her tea down and stood up. "I'll give Deb a try too, just in case Dad doesn't pick up."

"What about me?" I asked. Mum was speaking so calmly

that it had eroded some of my fear. I wanted to do something useful.

"Just sit tight, Martin."

"Really?"

"Just for a minute."

"Okay, fine." While staying put sounded appealing, I was disappointed not to be given a task. It would be a battle to sit and do nothing while Mum and Sarah went off to investigate, but I was too weary to argue.

What if something happened to them though? What if something happened to me?

I remained sitting while my family left the room, and with nothing else to do, my head filled with questions. What if our house had been beamed up by aliens? What if time had stopped and we were trapped here for all eternity?

Sarah came back into the living room, shaking her head and muttering to herself. At some point while she'd been gone she'd wiped the dry blood from her face, and it was a relief to see her face again. "Phone's still not working," she said. "Sounds like bees buzzing."

I frowned.

Mum came back into the room a second later, her expression telling a similar story. She slumped on the sofa and rubbed at her forehead.

"Mum?" I asked tentatively. "Are the doors still stuck?"

She sighed. "It's late. You should both get some rest."

"I'm not going upstairs. No way."

"Me neither," said Sarah.

"Then I want you both to lie down here and try to get some sleep. I'll watch over you until Dad gets home. We can't do anything else, can we?"

"I don't think I can sleep, Mum," Sarah said earnestly.

"Please try, sweetheart. I... I need to rest and I can't do

that if you kids are running around." She rubbed at her eyes, which were dark and swollen. I hadn't ever seen her look so tired. It worried me.

"Just sit down, Mum. I'll try and take a nap, okay?"

Sarah sighed. "Yeah, okay, me too."

"Thanks, kids."

Dad's armchair reclined, so I pulled the handle and my legs jumped up. Then I pushed back with my shoulders and lay almost flat. Like Sarah, I didn't think I could sleep, but as soon as I closed my eyes I began to drift. My body was heavy and my legs ached. In the last hour my heart had been racing a sprint. Everything could wait a little while.

When I next opened my eyes, someone was banging on the front door. It was light outside – not fully daytime, but getting close – and a weak blue light came in through a gap in the curtains. My eyes were fuzzy, and for a moment I was confused. Sarah was still asleep on the sofa, lying on her side and snoring loudly. Mum stood in the centre of the room, as disoriented as I was. "It-It must be your dad," she said. "He's late."

"Why is he banging at the door?" I asked, then answered my own question. "Oh yeah, it's stuck." I struggled to lean forward and fold down the recliner. It meant I arrived in the hallway several seconds after Mum. A blurry shape moved on the other side of the front door's glass pane that I hoped was Dad. When I heard his voice, I grinned.

"Someone's left their key in the door," he shouted. "I can't get in."

Mum stepped up to the glass. "Charlie, the door's jammed. We can't get out."

"Huh? Just take your key out of the lock."

"I can't. It's stu—" Mum turned the key easily. "Oh!"

The door opened and Dad appeared in his dirty blue

overalls. He seemed confused to see me standing there with Mum. "Sorry if I woke you both. Work ran late. I think Tim got fired."

Mum rubbed at her eyes and glanced at her watch. "It's almost six. Shit, I must have fallen asleep."

Dad frowned, probably surprised to hear Mum swearing. He let it go, though, and turned to close the door.

I screamed at him. "Don't!"

Dad flinched. "Wow, buddy, what's wrong?"

Mum put her hand on his shoulder and moved him aside. "Just trust us, you don't want to close the door."

"Why not exactly?"

Mum and I looked at one another. It would be very difficult to explain, but what choice did we have?

"You're not going to believe this, Dad, but I swear it's all true."

8

We explained the events of the night to Dad while frigid dawn turned to sunny morning, and when Sarah stirred from the sofa, we explained it all over again. He didn't believe us for one minute, of course, and his biggest question was why his family had suddenly banded together to tell such an insane story.

"We need to show him the door," said Sarah, leaning against the hallway bannister. The angle made her hip pop out, and I wondered when she had got so skinny.

"I don't want to go upstairs," I argued.

"But it's the only way he'll believe us."

Dad folded his arms, alternating between amused and concerned. Currently, he was smirking, like he suspected he was being tricked. If only that had been the case. "I think you better show me," he said. "Sooner I get my family back, the sooner I can get some sleep."

Mum folded her arms and nodded. "Sarah, stay with your brother and make sure this door doesn't close. Charlie, you come with me."

Dad shook his head and chuckled. Mum hesitated at the bottom of the stairs, and for a moment it looked like she wouldn't be able to go through with it. Then she started climbing one step at a time, Dad right behind her.

Sarah came and stood next to me by the still open front door, which I welcomed. I was chilly, afraid, and still dressed in only my boxer shorts, but I didn't want to move. People would start getting up for work soon, and I really didn't want them to see me, but it was better than the alternatives.

"We're going to end up in the newspapers," said Sarah. She still wore only a T-shirt and silk shorts, but she didn't seem as self-conscious as I was. "We'll be known as the crazy Birmingham family."

"They might make a movie," I said hopefully. "We could be in it."

"Get real. They'll lock us up the moment we start talking about ghost doors."

"Don't say that."

She frowned. "What?"

"Don't say *ghost*. I don't believe in ghosts."

"Then what do you think it is?"

"Aliens."

Sarah groaned. "Nice one, idiot. I'll believe in ghosts before I believe in aliens."

"Aliens are real. We can't be the only ones in the universe, can we?"

She didn't answer my question, just sniffed and turned away. We waited in silence until Mum and Dad came back downstairs. Mum had a hand to her mouth. Dad appeared even more confused.

"Well," said Sarah, "did you see it?"

Dad hopped off the bottom step and faced us. "I didn't see anything."

I looked past him. "Mum? What's up there?"

She had to blink before she could look directly at me. "Nothing. Just the same old wall that's always been there."

"Do I need to call a doctor?" asked Dad, still looking confused.

"I don't know," said Mum, and she sounded genuinely unsure. "This has been exhausting. I don't even know what day of the week it is. Charlie, I swear to you – we all swear – there was a strange room upstairs, and Courtney disappeared inside it. It happened."

Dad finally lost his confused smirk. He looked at Mum and only her, as if he couldn't trust anyone else to tell the truth. "Okay, something has clearly happened, but it's over now. Everything is normal. I'm here and everything is fine."

"Except Courtney," said Sarah. "He's still missing."

Dad scratched at his beard thoughtfully. "Let's see what today brings, okay? Maybe he'll turn up later with an explanation. If not... well, let's just see. It's half six in the morning and we should all get a couple of hours sleep. Things will be less confusing after a decent rest."

"I can't sleep any more," said Sarah. "I'm going to go to Deb's, if that's okay, Mum?"

"She'll still be sleeping."

"It's okay. Her window's at the front of the house. I'll throw pebbles until she hears me."

Dad grunted. "Break a window and you'll be in big trouble, young lady. I've got enough to pay out for this month." He then turned to me. "What about you, buddy? You look knackered. I'd like it if you went to bed for a while. Can you be brave and go upstairs?"

I shivered, still standing by the open front door. "You'll be up there too, right?"

"Right across the landing. Anything happens, I'll be right with you."

"I'll be there too," said Mum, rubbing at her dark eyes. "I can barely stay awake now that things have calmed down."

"Okay," I said. "I'll go back to bed, but can you wait until I fall asleep before you do?"

Mum gave me a cuddle. "Of course."

Sarah grunted. "I'm going to get my coat."

And so it was decided. The room upstairs had disappeared as suddenly as it appeared. The house I'd lived in my entire life was back to normal. No more crisis.

I just needed to see things with my own eyes.

And we needed to find out what happened to Courtney.

I waited for Dad to go upstairs and then followed. Sure enough, the door at the end of the landing was gone. Even so, I sought the safety of my room. I hurried in and slid beneath my covers, then stared at the ceiling until Mum came and tucked me in like a baby. "This will all be behind us soon," she told me, stepping back from my bed. "We'll probably never understand it, but at least it's over and we—" She stumbled in the centre of my room and looked down at her feet. "Oh, clumsy me. This goes on your shelf, right?"

I saw the Karazy Klown doll in Mum's hands and wondered how it had got there. "Put it next to my TV," I said. "It keeps falling off the shelf."

"Okay, sweetheart. I'll see you in a bit, okay?"

"Yeah, Mum. In a bit."

"Love you."

I rolled over on my side. "Love you too."

Mum left my room. I closed my eyes. Sleep pulled me in. I hadn't fully left slumber behind after waking up in Dad's recliner, so it was easy to find my way back. I settled down on a jet-black cloud and thought of nothing.

I awoke over five hours later – past noon, according to my clock – and I felt naughty for having slept in so late. I forgave myself by remembering that the night had been somewhat hectic, and that Dad had awoken me by returning home at six that morning.

In light of the new day, and having finally rested thoroughly, things seemed less frightening. My fear of the mysterious door now turned to curiosity, and even though it had happened mere hours ago, it felt as if it had never happened, like looking back on a bout of illness. The pain and distress feels endless in the moment, but when it finally breaks, you look back on it curiously, unable to fathom the misery you were in. You're just glad it's over.

Despite it feeling like a dream, I was anxious as I got out of bed and threw on some clothes. Part of me expected to see the strange door as soon as I poked my head out onto the landing, but when I stepped out, I saw only the normal cream-painted wall that had always been there.

How could I ever speak about last night to anyone?

Mike would laugh his head off at me.

But it had happened, I was sure of it. Last night, something visited our house. Something unnatural. Something *wrong*. My mind turned to Sarah, and to whether she was currently sharing the truth with Deb. Her best friend had once thought lamb was meat from a unique animal called a 'lamb'. It had taken twenty minutes to make her understand it was a sheep. Trying to make her understand about a mysterious door that appeared from nowhere would be an impossible task. I pitied Sarah if she even tried.

And had Courtney turned up yet? And if not, what did it mean? Were we responsible?

Dad was snoring loudly from his bedroom, so I tiptoed

downstairs and encountered Mum in the kitchen. She was staring out of the window above the sink.

"Mum, are you okay?"

She flinched. "Oh, Martin, you gave me a fright. Did you manage to sleep?"

"Yeah. The door is still gone."

From the way she bit her lip and failed to look at me, she clearly didn't want to talk about it – perhaps ever. "Do you want any breakfast? Although it's really lunchtime at this point."

I shook my head and stifled a yawn. "I haven't woken up properly yet. I'm just going to have a cup of tea and watch TV."

"I'll make it. You go sit down, honey."

"Okay, thanks. Mum, you, um, look upset."

She gave no reply, just resumed her staring. I slunk away into the living room to watch TV, settling on Channel Four because it was showing *The Mighty Ducks*. I'd seen the movie ten times already but I still loved it. In fact, I'd seen all three movies. The last one had sucked a bit though. They weren't kids any more.

I vaguely remembered the first time I had watched the original film. It had been with my dad – my real one. Mum always referred to him as 'Keith' if she ever mentioned him at all, and sometimes I wished he was still around so I could see what he looked like. My memories of him were murky, but none of them were bad. I knew Mum hated him, but I didn't know why. It was a confusing topic. Mostly I wished he was around so I could ask why he left. Mum never gave me a straight answer about it, and while she tried to speak nicely on the few occasions I asked about him, there had been one time when she'd been drinking at Diane's. She had told me he was a horrible man and that we were better off without him. Still, I wished he was still around so I could decide things for myself. If he were such a bad guy, I would see that for myself, right? But what if he wasn't a bad guy? What if he still wanted to be my dad?

But I already had a dad. Charlie had raised me the last four years, and he loved me. He was my dad.

There was a knock at the front door and I groaned. Whenever doors were involved lately, bad things happened. I got up from the sofa and shouted towards the kitchen. "I'll get it."

Mum didn't shout back a reply.

As usual, I could see the shape of the person knocking through the front door's glass pane. This time it was someone small. It could've been Sarah, but she would've let herself in with her key. I opened the door and grimaced when it turned out to be Diane. The wrinkled bags beneath her eyes had grown since the last time I'd seen her, and the stench she gave off was worse too. She always smelled of wee and alcohol. Once, I had overheard Mum telling Dad that her bladder had weakened due to constant drinking, and that she had to wear big pads in her knickers. It was gross, and whenever I spoke to her, I couldn't think of anything aside from that piss-soaked pad between her stick-thin legs. "Hi, Diane? Do you want my mum?"

"Oh, hello, Martin. I don't mean to be a bother. I just wanted to ask if I could borrow a couple of pounds."

Of course, just a couple of pounds. I wasn't sure she understood the word 'borrow', as she never paid Mum anything back. I failed to stop myself from releasing a tiny sigh, but Diane never seemed to notice when people were irritated by her – either that or she didn't care. I was about to shout for Mum, but someone else spoke and interrupted me.

"Diane, long time no see. How've you been?"

Diane turned on her wobbly legs and stared at the newcomer. Her face lit up. "My word, it's you! What a sight for sore eyes."

A stout, tough-looking man with brown hair moved out from behind Diane and gave her a hug. The very thought of doing so made me feel sick, but it didn't seem to bother him. "Did you just say you're short a few quid? Let's see what I've got."

The stranger reached a thick hand into his jeans and fished out a palmful of coins. Without superpowers, I couldn't work out at a glance how much was there, but I estimated at least five pounds, which was why I was shocked when he handed it all over to Diane.

Diane's face lit up as she took the hoard of coins. "Oh, Keith, you're an angel. It's so good to see you."

"You too, Diane."

Diane scurried away, so the stranger turned to me. I looked back at him, a single word spilling from my lips. "K-Keith?"

The man grinned, dark stubble around his open mouth. "Hello, Martin. You've grown."

Footsteps sounded on the floorboards behind me and I turned to see Mum. Her face fell in absolute horror. "What the hell are you doing here?" she demanded, and reached for the door.

"Nice to see you too, Sharon."

Mum's face distorted like shattered glass. "Fuck off, Keith! Fuck right off."

I gawped at my mother, staggered by her language. She was not pleased to see this man.

9

I didn't fully understand it at that moment, but the man standing on our doorstep was Keith Gable, my biological father. The man who I suddenly remembered teaching me to swim and ride a bike. A man who I remembered smiling more often than frowning. A man I was supposed to hate, yet didn't. Mum tried to close the door on him, but he blocked it with his foot.

"I'm here to see Martin and Sarah," he said. "I'm here to see my kids, Sharon."

"You have some nerve. They've been your kids for the last four years and you haven't wanted to know."

"Maybe I *would* have stuck around if you hadn't been so busy shacking up with a..." He shook his head and let out a breath. "I'm not here to fight, okay?"

"Good, then you can leave."

"Mum, what's going on? Is this... is this my dad?"

Mum's eyes glistened, and I felt ashamed – like I shouldn't have asked the question. She put an arm around me and pulled me close. "Martin, I..."

"Yes, I'm your dad, Martin. I've missed you. I can't

believe how big you've got. You look just like I did at your age. Is Sarah here? Sarah, are you in?"

"She's not here," my mum hissed. "Stop shouting."

I looked at the man, oddly angered by his familiarity and disregard for my mother. "What are you doing here?"

The question appeared to catch him – my dad – off guard, because he didn't have an answer. "I... It's just that... I needed to come and see you. I *had* to come."

"Why now? Why after being gone for years?"

That question seemed to confuse him even more, and his eyes went to Mum. "Has your mother never told you?"

I turned to Mum, but her eyes were locked on Keith. "How dare you? How fucking dare you? Get the hell out of here, you piece of shit."

Keith folded his arms and leant against the door frame. "I'm not going anywhere, Sharon. I have a right to see—"

"You gave up your rights nearly five years ago. Martin doesn't even know you."

"And whose sodding fault is that? I see you haven't changed one bit. You never could admit to being wrong."

The conversation was confusing. Things were being said that made me want to ask questions. Questions I wasn't sure I wanted the answers to. Mostly I was angry because this man was talking to my mum in a way I didn't like. I turned and waved a hand dismissively. "You're upsetting my mum, so you should go. This is our home."

Keith looked at me unkindly, and I wondered if this man could really be my dad. We had the same hair. "It used to be my home too until your mother—"

"I don't care. It's not your home now. Leave us alone."

I began to close the door, but Keith placed his arm out and blocked it. He looked back and forth between Mum and me. A mixture of emotions crossed his face, but after a brief standoff, he stepped back and sighed. "Martin, I know you and I have lost a lot of time, but I want to make it right. I want to be your dad again. Promise me we can speak soon, okay?"

"You'll have to ask my mum." I looked at her but did nothing to sway her answer. I would do whatever she wanted. Her anger had gone now and she was sad, eyes brimming to the point of spilling tears. Despite that, she smiled at me. "We'll talk about it, Martin, I promise. We'll talk about it."

I turned back to the doorway. "You heard her, Keith. We'll talk about it and get back to you."

Keith huffed, either amused or insulted, but he took another step back away from our door. "I suppose that's all I can ask for. I'll come back soon, okay? I just want to get to know you."

I pushed the door closed, and as soon as it shut, Mum collapsed in tears. I put my arms around her and she sobbed into my chest as if I were the adult and she the child. "I'm sorry, Mum."

She pulled away to look at me. "Don't you dare be sorry, Martin. You are not the one to blame. *He* is, you hear me?"

"I don't need to see him, Mum. He upsets you."

"Thank you for defending me, Martin, but he's your father and you have a right to know him if that's what you want. I might not like it, but it's true. I just can't believe he's suddenly turned up like this after so long."

I had no idea what I wanted. Keith seemed a bit of a *prick*, but he was also my real dad. Wouldn't it be stupid to refuse to see him if all he wanted was a relationship with me? "I'm not sure what I want, Mum. I can't even think about it right now."

"It's been a strange couple of days, hasn't it?"

I nodded. "It still feels like I dreamt it all. Are you okay, Mum?"

She kissed me on the cheek, something she rarely did nowadays, but instead of answering the question, she hugged me again and held onto me for a long time. I held her right back, because, for the first time in my life, home didn't feel safe.

A creaking sound made us both glance towards the stairs. Dad – Charlie – was stumbling down the steps, rubbing sleep from his eyes and yawning. When he saw us hugging at the bottom of the stairs, he frowned. "You both okay? What's happened now?"

Mum turned to him reluctantly. Her eyes were puffy with tears, and her cheeks were fatter than usual. "Charlie, we need to talk."

"Oh, that doesn't sound good."

"It's not, but just stay calm, okay?"

Dad's face fell as he realised his day was about to start badly.

And the days to follow would be even worse.

10

I spent the day in my room so Mum and Dad could talk in private. I blared out their bickering by turning up the volume on my TV. It was eight o'clock, and they were both still at it in the kitchen. Neither was pleased about Keith showing up, and I still wasn't entirely sure how I felt about it myself. I couldn't deny I was excited, but at the same time I was also afraid. Like he could hurt me somehow.

Nothing would make me feel any differently about Charlie – Dad – but meeting Keith had made me realise how awkwardly stuck together our current family was. For the first time, the colour of Charlie's skin seemed like an issue, because my real dad was white. It was all so confusing. The drone of my parents arguing downstairs didn't help. In fact, I was so preoccupied I almost forgot about what had happened the previous night.

Sarah hadn't forgotten though.

She'd come home around three o'clock and had headed straight to her room. I heard her sobbing soon after. Courtney hadn't turned up, that much was obvious, and any possibility he was playing some sort of prank was rapidly fading. The room had been real – impossible, but real – and it had done something to Courtney. Why had the idiot gone inside?

The main problem, with my sister crying across the hall and my parents arguing downstairs, was boredom. I'd been hiding out in my room for hours, not wanting to disturb anyone. But Saturday night TV was the worst. I needed to get out. Usually, I would hang out with Mike most of the weekend, but with all the drama at home I hadn't spoken to him for almost a week. There was so much I wanted to tell him.

So much I *couldn't* tell him.

I could tell him about Keith though. He wouldn't laugh at me for that.

I heard Sarah's sobbing from across the landing and I heard my parents arguing in the kitchen. I heard the balls dropping on the National Lottery.

Okay, that does it, I told myself. *I can't take any more.*

I got up and went across the hall, tapping lightly on Sarah's door.

"Go away," she yelled.

"It's Martin. Are you okay?"

I listened to my sister's stomping footsteps. I didn't expect her to open the door with a smile and, sure enough, she yanked it open with a scowl on her face. Her nose was bleeding I could barely believe it. "Jesus, Sarah, again?"

She had tears in her eyes and blood down the *Fugees* T-shirt she was wearing. "It's just a weak blood vessel. It keeps opening because of all this stress. Just leave me alone, Martin."

I genuinely didn't want to make her mad, so I half turned to leave, but she looked so broken that I needed to make sure she was okay. Sad people did things if you left them alone, right? I learned about it at school when Mrs Goggins had wheeled the TV in and played a video to our class. "Sarah, can I just... can I just ask about Courtney? Have you heard anything?"

Her eyes widened for a second like I had poked her, but then she shook her head slowly. A drop of blood spilled from her chin onto her bony shoulder. "I called a dozen people from Deb's house, but no one's heard anything. I called his mum too. I wish he would just turn up and be okay. Martin, what happened to him?"

"I don't know."

Sarah let out a hiss, then raised the bottom of her T-shirt to wipe the fresh blood from her face. The bottom of her pink bra peeked out over her ribs, which made me blush and look away. When I turned back, her T-shirt was back down and her face was a little cleaner. "This is so disgusting."

"You should see a doctor," I said. "It's not right. You're really thin, too, Sarah. Have you been forgetting to eat or something?"

"What? I'm fine. What about your stomach anyway? That isn't exactly right, is it?"

I stood straight, defying her attempts to ignore my concern. "My stomach's fine, so don't worry about—" My words faltered, and I doubled over, a sudden pain in my guts like an angry pike had woken inside of me. Sarah reached out and touched my arm. "Martin, what the hell? Are you playing around?"

"No, I feel really—" I puked all over the floor. "Oh, please, God, not again!" I puked a second time.

Sarah leapt back inside her room, barely avoiding getting spattered. She was seething with anger when I straightened back up to face her. "Martin, I swear to God... What is with you? Stop puking around me."

I wiped my mouth and groaned. "I-I'm sorry. I'm not doing it on purpose."

"Seems like you are. You were literally just saying you felt fine."

I heard footsteps on the stairs. The sight of my vomit all over the wall and carpet made me moan in misery. Mum and Dad would have a fit when they saw the mess. They would blame me for not making it to the toilet.

Mum appeared on the landing, hair tied back and her forehead sweaty. She focused on me, then on the wall – then she looked past me completely. She started to shake her head, eyes stretching wide. "No, no, it can't be."

I looked at Sarah, who seemed to be as confused as I was, then I looked back at my mum. "Mum, what is it?"

She carried on shaking her head. "No, no, no."

I turned, and my heart fluttered when I saw that the door had returned. It was only my disbelief that kept me from screaming. "Mum, it's back."

Mum reached out to us. "Both of you, get here."

Sarah broke first, racing past me towards the stairs. "Come on, idiot. Move!"

I staggered back on my heels, enchanted by the door. It was starting to open, letting out that same mocking *creak* that it had the previous night. Darkness filled the mysterious room inside, but as the landing light crept in, I saw it was still empty.

Until it wasn't.

As if forming from the air itself, a shape materialised in the middle of the room. A person. Maybe a monster?

Mum grabbed me and pulled me towards the stairs.

"No, wait!" I told her. "There's... there's someone inside. It's... It's... Oh God."

Sarah barged past me and started screaming. "Courtney! Courtney!"

Courtney staggered out onto the landing. He'd come back.

But he wasn't the same.

His eyes were shut tight and bleeding. He tried to speak, but only a mumbled blather came out. Both arms flailed as he crashed against the wall like a panicking moth. Sarah rushed to him and held him tightly, fighting his struggles and easing him down onto the carpet. There, on his knees, he started to moan like a zombie. Sarah looked back at us with absolute horror.

I wanted to say something, but I worried that if I dared move, my body would shatter into a thousand tiny pieces. I felt fragile and distant, once again away from my body as I watched the scene unfold before me. Courtney's eyes weren't closed; they were stitched shut. He wasn't mumbling; he was trying to talk, but his tongue was mangled and swollen. It appeared to have been sliced off. He was blind and unable to speak.

Sarah let out a scream so loud it hurt my ears, and I covered my mouth to keep from puking again. What the hell had happened to him in that room?

A thumping sounded on the stairs and Dad raced up to join us on the landing. "What's happening?" he asked breathlessly. "Who's screaming? Is Sarah okay? Is she..." His words caught in his throat as his eyes fell upon Courtney, and it took him several seconds to break out of his stupor and speak again. "W-We need to get this boy to a hospital. Right now!"

Sarah was hyperventilating, tears, snot, and blood all

over her face. "Help him, Dad. Help him. He came out of the room like this."

Courtney had stopped flailing and was now resting silently like an animal giving in to shock. One time, our car had hit a cat on our way home from the supermarket, and it had lain by the side of the road in the exact same way Courtney was lying now, breathing heavily but otherwise completely still. Dying.

This was too much. What I was seeing was too much. I felt like it was going to scar me forever, like I was standing too close to a flame. "Dad, what are we going to tell the hospital?"

"I don't know, Martin. Just help me carry him. He needs our help."

I did as I was told, but as I would later find out, Courtney was beyond help.

We all were.

Courtney had resumed his panic by the time we bundled him into the car, and it took both me and Sarah to calm him as we held him across our laps in the back seat. His moaning, along with the screeching tyres of our speeding Vauxhall Cavalier, were the only sounds as we raced to the hospital. Dad almost drove right through the entrance of A&E.

Then things had got complicated. Seeing Courtney's horrific state, several nurses rushed to our aid, speeding him away in a wheelchair. Then a doctor questioned us, but instead of a white-coated gentleman with pens in his top pocket, what we got was a brawny young man in an open-collared white shirt with his sleeves rolled up. He spoke with a strange accent, but was white, so I assumed he was French or German. I was studying French at school, and I considered throwing out a few words to see what happened. Then I realised I could say little beyond 'Hello' and 'My name is...'

Bonjour, je m'appelle Martin Gable.

"I am Doctor Renbert. Is the boy you brought in tonight a member of your family?"

My dad answered. "No."

"He's my boyfriend," said Sarah. "His name is Courtney Hodge."

The doctor nodded. "Okay, *ja*. Can you please provide my nurse with full details, along with those of his family if you know them?"

Dad nodded. "Of course. I'm sure Sarah has all that. Is he going to be okay? What happened to him?"

"I could ask you the same thing. What was your name again, sir?"

"Charlie Ademale. This is my family."

The doctor studied us suspiciously for a moment, but then nodded. "To answer your question, from what I can tell, the boy you brought in has been tortured. His tongue has been severed and his eyes removed. I'm yet to confirm it, but I believe him to be deaf also. I'm assuming he wasn't always so, *ja*?"

Sarah started hyperventilating, flapping her arms like a bird. Mum moved her away so she couldn't hear any more of the grizzly details. Dad put a hand to his face. "No, he wasn't deaf. I don't understand why someone would do these things to an innocent boy."

"His life is irreparably changed," said Dr Renbert in that strange accent of his. I had decided he sounded more German than French, but I still wasn't certain. "How did you discover the boy in such a state?"

Dad glanced at me and swallowed. This was what I'd been worrying about. What on earth did we say? What would happen if we spoke about the room? I started to fret.

The men in black are going to seize our house and make us disappear, I worried to myself. The Government probably knows all about things like this and covers them up. What if we speak about the room and it isn't there when the police look? They'll call us liars and blame Courtney's injuries on us. They'll lock us up in prison.

Doctor Renbert cleared his throat. "I asked you a question, Mr Ademale."

Dad stuttered and failed to speak again, so I answered for him. "Courtney came to our door, banging his fists and moaning. It was scary, so I shouted for my mum and dad."

Dad licked his lips and looked at me. It clearly upset him that I was lying, but I couldn't let him tell the truth. The truth was impossible to tell. After a moment, he gradually accepted that fact. "Yes, Courtney just turned up out of the blue. We're all in shock about it. He's a good kid, but we don't know him that well. Who knows how he got into this situation."

The doctor nodded. "*Ja*, well, hopefully we shall find out. Okay, thank you for that information, Mr Ademale. I'm afraid we have contacted the police and they will want to speak with you too."

I watched my dad deflate, but he didn't lose his cool. He must have expected this. "Of course. We're not going anywhere."

"Good, please get those details to my nurse concerning Courtney's family as soon as possible"

"Right away. Thank you, Doctor."

The doctor hurried away, his black trainers squeaking on the shiny floor. I turned to Dad, who kept his eyes on the man until he disappeared around a corner. "He talks funny," I said, "and he's young. Is he really a doctor?"

"He's South African." He said it with a hint of distaste but didn't elaborate. He put his hand on my back and moved me towards a row of plastic chairs where Sarah and Mum

had already sat down. Sarah was a mess. Mum was morti-
fied. I was silent.

Dad knelt in front of Sarah and put a hand on her knee.
"They need you to give Courtney's details at the desk, sweetheart. They want to contact his family."

Sarah lifted her head away from Mum's chest. "We did
this. We did this to him."

"Sweetheart, that's not true – and I'm not sure we should
be saying it. Something terrible has happened to Courtney
and the police are going to get involved. We need to be very
careful about what we say."

It relieved me to hear Dad say that. He was taking charge
of the situation and that was good. Sarah didn't seem to
think so though because her face devolved into a scowl. "Is
that all you care about? Making sure we don't get into trouble? Courtney's life is over and all you can do is think about
yourself."

"Sweetheart, I'm thinking about us all."

Sarah batted his hand off of her knee. "I'm not your
sweetheart. You're not my fucking dad."

Dad reared back like a startled horse. Once he recovered, he placed both hands on his hips and glared. "Sarah,
do not use language like that, do you hear me?"

"Fuck you!"

"Sarah! You will not—"

Mum put a hand up. "Just leave her, Charlie. Now isn't
the time."

"What? Sharon, we need to have our heads screwed on
or this is going to get worse. Do you understand how serious
this is?"

"Of course I do! Charlie, our entire life has turned to shit
in a matter of days. I feel like we've been cursed; that we're
in a hole we can't get out of and it keeps getting deeper. But

snapping at Sarah won't make anything better, will it? Give her a minute and I'll take her to the desk to give Courtney's details. God help his poor parents."

I hadn't even thought about that. Courtney had a family and this would destroy them. If I'd lost my sight and hearing, as well as my ability to talk, Mum would lose the plot. She'd been a nightmare when I'd caught chicken pox.

Dad finally got the message and wandered off towards a row of vending machines. I didn't know whether to follow him. Was I supposed to leave Sarah alone too? I didn't want to be in the way.

Mum made eye contact with me. "Sit down, honey. Save your energy."

"Is Sarah okay?"

Mum nodded, but Sarah glared at me. "Of course I'm not okay, you idiot. How could you even ask that?"

"Sorry."

Mum shushed us and we fell silent. Dad got himself a coffee from the vending machine across the hall and it annoyed me when he didn't offer to get anything for the rest of us. Instead, he moved away to read the colourful health notices pinned to a large cork board. Sarah argued with Dad often, but I had never witnessed her speak to him like she had today. To make things worse, Mum didn't even seem to be on his side about it.

I wanted to make sure he was okay, so I got up and walked across the waiting room. When Dad sensed my presence, he glanced over his shoulder, but then he went back to examining the noticeboard. He wasn't in a mood to talk, so I didn't say anything. I stood next to him, examining the various notices.

BEAT GERMS. WASH YOUR HANDS.
OVER 60? GET YOUR FREE FLU JAB.

DENNIS THE MENACE DOESN'T DO DRUGS.

Realising I wasn't going to go away, Dad cleared his throat and spoke to me. "So, how are you feeling about Keith turning up? Must be a lot going through your head."

I stared at him hard. "It's all because of the room. It made everything horrible."

"Martin, you heard what I said to your sister. We need to be careful about what we say."

I nodded, but my mouth was defiant. "You saw the room. You saw it when Courtney came out."

"I don't know what I saw. I was focused on Courtney."

"Dad..."

"Martin, please? Let's not speak about it, okay? We should wait and see what happens. There's a lot going on, but I'm just trying to protect us all. That's my job." A bulge bobbed up and down his throat. Something had upset him. He muttered, "I'm your father."

I wasn't good at showing my feelings – I always felt so embarrassed – and if Sarah was anywhere near, she would make fun of me. "I'm sorry how Sarah spoke to you. I don't care what she thinks, you're our dad."

He managed a smile, but it wasn't real. He had these great big eyes where you could see all the little red veins. The veins seemed to grow when he was upset. "Keith's your real dad, Martin, and he wants to get to know you. Sarah, too, most likely. Things are going to be okay, but your mum... She went through a lot with Keith and it took her a long time to get over it. We need to be there for her, even if you start seeing Keith."

"I'm not sure I even want to. You've been my dad since I was six. Where was he?"

"Honestly, I have no idea, but I won't stand in your way if you want to see him. It's your right, Martin. Your mum and I agree on that much. You should get to know him if that's what you want."

"I don't want to upset you."

He put a hand on my back and pulled me against his side. "Don't you worry about that, buddy. I'll be okay as long as you're happy, okay?"

"Dad, is Courtney going to be okay? I can't... I keep trying to imagine not being able to see or hear or speak. Will the doctors be able to help him, because if not...? It makes me want to cry. It makes me want to cry because it's so horrible. Courtney was kind to me."

Dad's throat bulged, and he cleared his throat to shift a phlegmy blockage. Then he turned and leant against the noticeboard. His eyes were brimming with tears, mixing with the red veins and making his whites appear pink. "If anything like that ever happened to you, Martin, I don't know what I'd do. What happened to Courtney is heartbreaking and terrifying and every parent's worst nightmare, but that doesn't mean any bad will happen to you though. You're a good boy, Martin. You're sensitive and kind, and that only makes what's going on harder. I don't understand what's going on, but I promise to keep you safe. As long as we stick together, we'll make it through whatever this is."

I nodded, then glanced back across the waiting room to where Mum was still sitting cradling Sarah. "Then why are we standing over here on our own, Dad?"

He gave a chuckle. "Good point. Come on, let's grab some snacks and go back."

12

As a family, we sat and ate our snacks in silence. Sarah had stopped crying, and although she didn't apologise for the way she had spoken to Dad, she was kinder. She even shared her prawn cocktail crisps. I had smoky bacon, Mum salt and vinegar.

The police arrived thirty minutes later. Dad tensed up at the sight of them. I'd never been particularly afraid of getting in trouble before, but I felt vulnerable now as I watched the two officers stomp around the hospital, talking to various members of the staff and making notes. For the first time in my life, I felt the police were out to get me. Their job was to punish people, and when they saw the state of Courtney, they would want to hold someone responsible. As little as it made sense, that was us.

We were responsible.

It happened in our house.

My heart drummed in my chest as I imagined life inside a cell surrounded by scary, violent people who would make my life miserable. I imagined never seeing my parents again.

You're getting carried away, Martin, I told myself. Get up and take a walk.

"I'm just going to stretch my legs," I said, standing up and arching my back.

"Huh?" Dad was still eyeballing the officers, who were now standing at the reception desk talking to a nurse. When they glanced our way, he lowered his gaze and started fiddling with his fingers. "Oh, um, okay. Don't speak to anyone though, okay, Martin?"

Mum gave me a reassuring smile. "And don't go far, honey, okay?"

"Okay."

I don't know what possessed me, and perhaps it was fate, but instead of giving the police a wide berth, I strode directly towards them. Despite seeing them as a threat, I was also angry that they were making my dad so uncomfortable. They'd been in the hospital for a while but were yet to speak with us. It felt like they were letting us worry on purpose. I wasn't quite brazen enough to stand right next to them, but I knelt close by, pretending to tie my shoelaces. Once I realised they weren't paying me attention, I became rather pleased with myself. I was Martin Gable, secret agent.

"Is there no way at all of communicating with the patient?" I heard one officer say. He was a hair taller than his colleague and sported a goatee beard like Stone Cold. He was thin rather than muscly however.

"I'm afraid it's too soon for us to think about that," replied a nurse. "Right now, the patient's care is our only concern. I understand you need answers but—"

"We need to catch whatever monster did this. I've never seen anything like this in my entire career."

"Nor have any of us here," said the nurse a little testily.

She clearly didn't like being spoken over. "As soon as we can assist you, we shall."

The officer clapped a hand on the reception desk and the sudden noise made me flinch. "See that you do so, ma'am. In the meantime, we'll question the family who brought him in. That's them over there, correct?"

Fearful of my cover being blown, I stood and turned my back on the officers, hurrying to reach a place out of sight. In the corner of my eye, I saw the nurse point at my family. It was finally happening. We were about to be questioned.

My body started to tremble and I needed a wee. Fear flooded my system as I hurried to the corner of the waiting room and took a spot where I could hide and watch the officers approach my family. Dad stood and offered a handshake. The goateed officer obliged.

That was a good sign, right?

I wanted to join Mum, Dad, and Sarah, but I couldn't bring myself to move. It was horrible; so horrible that I wanted to curl into a ball and cry. Why was this happening to us?

"You brought that boy in, didn't you?" said a voice. "The boy with no eyes."

I flinched, bumping the back of my head against the wall. I turned to my left and saw a large man sitting on a nearby chair against the adjoining wall. He was old but not frail. In fact, he looked tough and strong. Deep-set wrinkles streaked his face and a pudgy scar interrupted the jet-black stubble on his chin. All this I saw beneath the brim of a dark blue baseball cap that didn't suit his age nor appearance. "W-Who are you?"

The man was holding a deck of cards that he was shuffling back and forth in his hands. "My name is Thomas Quick. I've just arrived, but I've been watching your family."

I shuffled along the wall, feeling threatened and wanting to get away. "W-Why?"

"Because someone logged a new admission in the system that piqued my interest. A badly mutilated boy, blinded and made mute. I paid an orderly to point out the people who brought him in, and that turned out to be you."

"I'm going to get my dad."

"Hold your horses, I'm not here to hurt you, boy. I want to help." He stared at me with ghostly blue eyes that were so light that they seemed washed out. He whipped the pack of cards from one hand to the next without even looking. "And trust me, you need help."

I stopped shuffling along the wall. Could this man actually be able to help? If so, I needed to listen. "Tell me what you mean or I'm going to get someone."

The man removed his baseball cap and revealed a head full of straggly grey hair. A patch was missing above his left ear like he'd been burned. "I work for a very old organisation called the Sphere of Zosimus. Its history goes back all the way to the Roman Empire."

I knew lots about the Roman Empire. I had a textbook with a wicked picture of a hundred armoured soldiers lining up with their shields in a row, with even more above their heads. It looked like a giant tortoise shell, and they did it to keep arrows or rocks from hitting them. I tried to think of the proper word to describe it and was impressed when it came to me.

Testudo.

"I know about Romans," I said, "but I've never heard about the Sphere... Sphere of..."

"Zosimus," said the stubbled stranger. "He was a pagan historian, but that's not important. Our organisation is large and powerful, yet most people have no idea we exist. That's by design."

I nodded as if I understood, but I didn't at all. "What does your company do?"

"Not company – *organisation*. There are no profits involved. But to answer your question, we protect people."

I glanced at the two police officers now deep in conversation with my family. "You mean like them?"

"I suppose so, except we help in situations where the police can't. Your family is in trouble, isn't it, Martin?"

I nodded, then punched myself in the leg for trusting a stranger with the truth – a stranger who somehow knew my name. "My dad will take care of it."

I moved to walk away, but the man stood up and towered over me like a giant from *The BFG*. There were more scars on his neck, like someone had once tried to cut off his head. Instead of cowering, I stood my ground. It felt important not to show fear – even against a terrifying stranger like this one.

"You've brought something home, boy. I can't tell you what it was because it takes many forms, but it's in your possession, which means your entire family is in mortal danger."

Mortal danger? What did that even mean?

I started to walk away, keeping my shoulders straight and my stride long. The guy was obviously crazy.

There was whole lot of crazy in my life lately.

"Don't wish for anything," the man barked after me, his voice a few decibels below a shout. "Not even in your head. Every time you make a wish, you have to pay for it. Your injured friend is currency used to clear debt."

People in the waiting room started to look our way, and many frowned to see a young boy being accosted by a scruffy old man. The stranger – Thomas Quick, he had said – seemed to realise this because he gathered a long woollen coat from the back of his chair and put it on. He placed the playing cards in an inside pocket. "I'll come and see you soon, boy. Accept my help when I do."

Dad shouted over to me then, but not because he'd realised I was in trouble. "The police want to talk to you, Martin," he said. "Come over here, please."

I glanced back towards the stranger, but he was already halfway towards the exit, his long coat flapping behind him. It struck me as odd he was even wearing one in the middle of summer. He must have had ice in his veins.

Weirdo.

I took my time walking over to the waiting police officers. Having to cross the distance between us made me feel guilty, like a naughty child, and by the time I reached the seating area my cheeks were burning hot.

"Hello, Martin," said the officer with the goatee. "My name is PC Dorrens. This is PC Morrison. We'd just like to ask you a few questions about your friend, Courtney."

"He's not my friend," I said, and from the frown on the officer's face, I realised I had said it in an oddly defensive way. I'd seen enough TV shows to know that the police tried to trick you with their questions, so I had been defensive from the get-go. "I just mean he's my sister's boyfriend. I only really met him for the first time last night."

"You saw Courtney last night?"

I glanced at Dad, trying to get a clue on how to answer. His expression gave me nothing, so I had to just answer on my own. "He was with my sister last night for a bit. I wasn't paying much attention because the wrestling was on."

PC Dorrens smiled. "My son loves wrestling too. Who's your favourite?"

"DX."

The office nodded, but I suspected he knew nothing about wrestling. Maybe he didn't even have a son. His partner looked at the notepad he was holding and spoke without making eye contact. "What time did Courtney leave your home last night, Martin?"

"About eight o'clock."

"Your sister said nine, could that be more accurate?"

"She'd know better than me. Like I said, I wasn't paying attention."

"Fair enough. At any point last night did Courtney seem upset or angry? Troubled in any way?"

I shook my head. "He got me a Big Mac from McDonalds and then asked me to get my sister's CDs from the lounge. He seemed fine. I like him. I don't understand why this happened." Tears teased at my eyes, but it wasn't a tactic to make the police leave me alone. It was an actual surge of sadness that suddenly hit me, unleashed by having to talk about the worst events of my short life.

And it was a hundred times worse for Courtney.

"So you have no idea where Courtney might have gone last night after leaving your house?" PC Dorrens glanced sideways to look at the notes his colleague had just made.

"I have no idea. Mum got home from our next-door neighbour's house and then asked Courtney to go home."

Both officers looked at Mum, who shifted in her seat and looked down at her hands. What had I said wrong?

PC Morrison stared at me for a moment. "That's strange, because your mother told us that when she got back from the neighbour's house, Courtney had already left and that you were in bed with a stomach bug. How are you feeling, by the way?"

"I'm fine. It was just a quick thing from some bad chicken." I shrugged, trying to figure out what to say next. It seemed best to just act like I didn't know anything. "I assumed Courtney left when Mum got home because that's usually when Sarah's boyfriends have to go. Maybe he left earlier than that, but it was around the same time. Again, I wasn't really paying attention."

"Because you were watching wrestling? But you were ill?"

"I was resting. Trying to feel better."

"Okay, so Sarah's boyfriends usually leave when your mum gets back from the next-door neighbour's. Does your sister have a lot of boyfriends?"

"Hey," said Sarah. "Courtney and me are going out. There's no one else."

The officer turned to her. "Any ex-boyfriends who might be jealous, Sarah? Have you broken up with anyone recently?"

Sarah froze, making it obvious there was an interesting answer to his question. Mum saw the situation escalating and intervened. "She recently broke up with a boy named Darren, but he has nothing to do with this. He wouldn't hurt a fly."

PC Morrison tapped his notepad with his pencil. "All the same, we'll need some details. Do you have his address?"

Mum shook her head. "Sarah, do you?"

"I know his phone number, if you want that?"

"Yes, please," said the officer.

Sarah recited Darren's phone number, then lowered her head into her hands.

The officers turned their attention back on me. I felt like they were going to snap handcuffs on us any minute and lead us away. They were just waiting for me to say the wrong thing and land us all in trouble. How much longer did I need to keep answering questions?

PC Dorrens cleared his throat. "Okay, Martin, you told the doctor earlier that you were the one who found Courtney. Can you describe what happened? What time was it exactly?"

I said I didn't know, which felt like a safe answer. "We came here right away, but I don't remember what time it was. I was in the living room watching *a film* and someone started banging on the door. It was loud and it made me jump, so I ran to open it."

"What film?"

"Um, the *Mighty Ducks*."

"If the banging worried you, Martin, why didn't you get one of your parents?"

"Because it scared me in a different way. Like, I thought maybe it was Sarah, and she was in trouble."

"Why would she be in trouble?"

I sensed more traps being laid, and I realised that *the Mighty Ducks* had been on during the afternoon, not when I had claimed to have opened the door to Courtney. Would they catch my lie? "It's just a rhetorical thing, isn't it?" I said. "I didn't mean she was actually in trouble, just that I was worried by the banging on the door."

"I think you mean hypothetical," said PC Dorrens, "but I understand what you mean. Please go on, Martin."

"Well, I um, opened the door and Courtney was there. He was on his knees, moaning in pain. I didn't understand what was wrong, so I called out for Mum, who was in the kitchen."

"She was in the kitchen?"

"Yeah."

"Didn't she hear the banging? You said it was loud enough to scare you? How large is your home?"

Dad spoke up. "What does that have to do with anything?"

PC Dorrens shrugged a single shoulder. "If you lived in a six-bedroom mansion, it would make sense not to hear the front door from the kitchen. Do you live in a large home, Mr Ademale?"

Dad sniffed. "I wouldn't call it that."

PC Dorrens turned back to me, nodding slowly. "So, why didn't your mum come to the door when the banging started, Martin?"

Should I tell them it was because she was in a weird daze, standing in front of the sink and staring out of the window? A daze that had started after a strange door had appeared on our landing.

"I had my headphones in," said Mum, and it sounded completely plausible, despite the fact I had never seen her wear a pair of headphones in my life. "I thought I heard something, but it wasn't until Martin started shouting that I realised someone was at the door."

PC Morrison wrote something on his notepad. PC Dorrens stroked his goatee and seemed to think about things. "That makes sense then. Okay, well, you all should get yourselves home. It's getting late and Courtney's parents are on the way. Probably best they're given some privacy. This will be a terrible shock to them."

"I can only imagine," said Mum, shaking her head. "It's just awful."

"I want to stay here," said Sarah. "I need to be here for Courtney."

"There's nothing you can do for him right now," said PC

Morrison. "I suggest you leave a number where the nurses can contact you and wait for them to call."

"Yeah, because it's that easy to sit and wait." She sounded as if she had never heard anything so stupid. In fact, I was pretty sure she was going to call the officer an idiot. I was glad when she didn't.

Mum patted her knee. "You can go spend the day with Deb tomorrow, honey. I'm not having you at home crying yourself silly. You need to be around your friends."

Sarah rolled her eyes and shrugged.

Both police officers smiled at my mum, suggesting they agreed with her parenting. Then they both looked at me. PC Dorrens spoke. "Thank you for answering our questions, Martin. Try not to think too much about what's happened, okay? I don't want you having nightmares."

I nodded, but I was definitely going to have nightmares – nightmares about being trapped inside my own head, unable to see or hear or speak. Living in a world of darkness and silence. It made me want to scream.

"You all take care," said PC Morrison. "We'll be in touch."

Dad stood and shook hands with both of them. "Thank you, officers."

Once they'd gone, Dad stood and put his arms around me. "Good job, Martin. It's over now. We can all go home."

"Yeah," I agreed, but the thought of going home wasn't all that appealing; and Dad was naive if he thought things were over. There was more going on than we understood, that much was clear. I hadn't even told him about Thomas Quick, the stranger who warned we were all in danger.

The stranger who would turn out to be right.

13

A nd so we left Courtney at the hospital: blind, deaf, and with secrets he couldn't tell. If we'd known what we were up against, we would've gone home and torched our house, but even that wouldn't have saved us. We had no idea what we were dealing with.

How could we?

Upon leaving the hospital, Dad took us to a late-night cafe on a nearby road. Nobody said it, but we didn't want to go home. We didn't want to go upstairs. We didn't want to see if it was still there – the room. The dangerous thing in our house.

I had become certain that whatever had invaded our home was vile, an unnatural presence that meant us harm. Aliens, ghosts, demons... I didn't know, but my innocence had been supplanted by the revelation that the monsters under my bed were real. As places of spiritual awakening went, a greasy, smoky old cafe made an odd location.

Dad left our table to use the toilet, and a miserable waitress bought our food during his absence. We were already eating by the time he returned. Mum and Dad had ordered ham and eggs while Sarah's plate had a row of sausages she barely touched. I'd gone for a warm tuna baguette, which I devoured in massive bites.

Dad raised his eyebrows. "Wow, buddy. You starving?"

I spoke with my mouth full. "Yeah. When did we last eat?"

Sarah nudged her plate away, only half a sausage gone from the line-up. "I think I'm getting a cold."

Dad frowned. "Then food is the best thing. You need to eat, sweetheart."

"I can't. I'm too upset about Courtney."

I put down my half-eaten baguette and winced at the thought of his injuries. Suddenly I didn't feel so hungry any more. "I still can't believe what happened to him."

Mum reached forward and grabbed our hands across the table. "It's been a long day, kids. Things will get better, I promise."

"No shadow lasts forever," said Dad. "My grandmother used to tell me that all the time."

"I don't want to go home," said Sarah, broaching the subject none of us wanted to talk about. "I never want to go back."

"It's our home," said Dad. "Where else can we go?"

"A hotel."

Dad grimaced. "You think we can afford that? We'd be broke in less than a week."

"God, I am so sick of having no money. Mum, why did you even get with him?"

I was shocked by my sister's spitefulness, and my mouth fell open. Dad looked down and prodded his food with his fork. He was clearly tired of fighting.

Mum let go of our hands and sat back in her creaky plastic seat. She stared at my sister for a good long minute until Sarah eventually rolled her eyes and shrugged. "Take a picture, why don't you?"

"I'm so disappointed in you, Sarah. I know you haven't always had it easy, but I'm genuinely let down by the woman you've become. I had hoped for more."

I expected Mum to continue, but that was it. She just lowered her head and resumed eating. Sarah frowned, seemingly as confused as I was that she hadn't been torn apart. She kept her mouth closed.

Eventually Dad broke the tension. "We'll stay in a hotel tonight, but tomorrow we'll have to go home. I'm not sure what I saw upstairs exactly, or what happened to Courtney, but we'll figure it all out. We'll get answers."

Sarah deflated like a balloon, and she even gave Dad a smile, but Mum remained impassive, chewing chips one after another, almost robotically. It gladdened me that we wouldn't be going home. At least not yet.

"There was a man at the hospital," I said. "He was weird and scary, but…"

Mum put down the chip she had been about to pop in her mouth and stared at me. "But what, Martin? What man are you talking about?"

"He told me his name was Thomas Quick, and he seemed to know what was happening. He said we had brought something home with us and that we were in danger."

Sarah scoffed. "Liar."

"I'm not lying. He was wearing a baseball cap and had a big scar on his chin."

Sarah rolled her eyes.

Dad shook his head. "Martin, why on earth didn't you tell me? We should've told the police if he threatened you."

"He didn't threaten me. I think he was trying to warn me.

He said he would come see me soon and that I should accept his help."

Mum started laughing, and at such a high volume that the grumpy waitress behind the counter glanced over at us before returning to the newspaper spread out in front of her. "I feel like I'm on drugs. Charlie, we need to go back to the police and tell them everything."

"Are you joking? *Machende!* You want to tell them there's a magic room in our house that ate Sarah's boyfriend?"

Sarah put her face into her hands and started sobbing.

Mum pushed her plate away and turned to Dad beside her. "A stranger approached our son, Charlie, and said he would come back."

"If anyone tries to hurt Martin, they'll have me to deal with, but let's not overreact until we understand what's going on. If we go to the police with half a story, it'll end badly. The guy was probably just a loon."

"So what do we do then? Wait for the next bad thing to happen? We're cursed, Charlie. Like Martin said, we brought something home with us."

"I didn't say that. The man did."

Dad sighed. "A man named Thomas Quick? Look, this is... Let's just find a place for tonight and see what tomorrow brings. I don't know what else to do. If we're set on speaking with the police, then we'll make a plan for exactly what we're going to say. Right now, it's late and we're tired. It's not a good time to make decisions."

"Fine," said Mum. "I agree. Let's go find a hotel. The Vixen is near here. Maybe it won't be too expensive."

I popped a chip in my mouth and swallowed it whole. Before I slid out from the table, Sarah lurched forward and grabbed a serviette from the table's dispenser. "God's sake," she hissed. "My nose is bleeding again."

"That's it!" said Mum. "First thing in the morning, we're getting you checked out by a doctor. This can't be right."

"I'll go pay the bill," said Dad, getting up and hurrying to the grumpy waitress.

I stayed sitting, no longer wanting to get up. It could have been a coincidence, but my tummy hurt. It seemed that whenever Sarah had a nosebleed, I got sick.

It might have been a coincidence.

But it wasn't.

14

I've always had a thing about hotel beds. Whatever the size or quality of mattress, I sleep like a log, and that night at the Vixen was no different. Sleep came easily just minutes after I tucked myself beneath the crisp sheets of the hotel's double bed. My slumber was so deep that when I woke up, it took me several seconds to realise where I was.

Sarah had shared the bed with me but apparently got up first. I heard a hairdryer blaring, which meant she had already taken a shower. I didn't want to get out of bed yet. The events of the past couple of days hadn't yet fully come back to me and I wanted to make the most of being safe and cosy.

I lay there for five more minutes until Sarah appeared and attempted to rouse me. Fully dressed, she was brushing the tangles from her hair. "Get up, Martin. Mum says we can go back to the hospital and check on Courtney."

I shuffled up the bed and leant against the headboard. "Has anyone called? Do we know anything?"

She stopped grooming her hair and stared at the brush,

rolling it back and forth in her hand. "Mum called them first thing, but they wouldn't tell us anything. We're not family."

"That's stupid. We're the ones who brought him in."

"Maybe his parents don't want us to know. I'll go find them when I get there. They need to hear how much I love Courtney."

"You love him?"

"I think so."

"Wow."

She shrugged. "Either way, I'm going to help him through this. I won't abandon him."

Sarah wasn't the kindest person, but she seemed to mean what she said. But how would it even work? Courtney couldn't see or hear, or speak either. What relationship did she expect to have with him? What relationships could Courtney ever hope to have with anyone ever again? It sucked so badly. He was a good guy and his life was ruined. It would probably have been better if he had died. In fact, I wished he...

No! I stopped myself. Don't wish for anything. That's what Thomas Quick said. Don't wish. Don't even think it. I had wished for a Big Mac and Sarah had wished for Courtney to be at our house. Stupid, simple wishes, but...

Had we caused this?

"Sarah," I said, my mind buzzing with a dozen thoughts, "this'll sound really strange, but don't wish for anything, okay?"

She had resumed brushing her hair, but once again she stopped and looked at me. "What d'you mean?"

"The man who spoke to me at the hospital mentioned wishes. I think bad things happen when we wish for stuff."

"What are you talking about, idiot?"

I rubbed sleep from my eyes so I could focus on her

fully. "Look, Sarah, just promise me you won't make any wishes, okay? Please?"

Her lips parted like she was going to insult me again, but instead she shrugged. "Okay, fine. I promise I won't blow out any candles or make any wishes. Just get up, will you?"

I relaxed against the pillow. Things suddenly felt a little less dangerous. "Okay, I just need one more minute."

"Of course, I've been wishing for Courtney to get better, but that doesn't count, right?"

Lightning struck my spine and I grew light-headed. Whether fear or something supernatural, I felt one thing clearly. Dread. Like hot metal dripping on the back of my neck.

"Sarah, I don't think you should've done that."

She rolled her eyes at me. "Idiot."

I got dressed in a daze, staring at the wall the entire time. My thoughts crunched to a halt and I waited for the next bad thing to happen – because I knew it was coming.

There was a knock at the door.

Sarah opened the door to Dad. His dark skin had gone a peculiar shade of grey, and his big eyes were puffy and red. He obviously hadn't slept a wink.

"You both ready?" he asked us, leaning against the door frame and yawning. "If we get a move on, we can go get breakfast somewhere."

Sarah tossed the brush down on the dressing table and shuffled into her trainers. I quickly got ready, throwing on the previous night's clothes, and then joined them both at the door.

We walked down the corridor until we reached the reception area where Mum was already sitting staring out of the window. I sat in a comfy chair beside her, glad when she noticed me and smiled. Her eyes looked sore – like she'd spent the night crying – and her shoulders were sagging lower than I'd ever seen them. It was frightening, seeing my mother so weak. Before I was born she'd been a nurse, and I knew she planned on being one again some day. She was the one who always dealt with our cut knees, bad breakups, and naughty behaviour without batting an eyelid. She was the one who kept us all safe, happy, and fed. But she had gone somewhere now, and every time I looked at her it was like a part of her was missing. It frightened me more than I wanted to admit.

Dad went to the reception desk to check us out. A sign on the wall said the *Vixen* had once been a coaching inn, but with its horrible blue carpets and white-painted doors, it didn't make me think of a coaching inn at all. Behind the reception desk, a stuffed fox stood beside a photograph of the hotel staff. On duty today was a young woman with bright red lipstick and a tight ponytail, and she smiled at Dad as he leant on the desk and pulled out his wallet.

Sarah joined me and Mum by the window, but she didn't speak. It was nice to sit quietly in the morning sunlight cast through the windows and I was in no hurry to leave. I really didn't want to visit the hospital again, but I knew I had to. Courtney was there because of us.

Dad returned, stuffing his wallet back into his jeans. He was about to say something but the phone rang at reception and interrupted him, so instead of speaking, he just smiled and nodded to the doors. *Let's go.*

We got up and started to head out, and when the receptionist called after us, none of us registered it. It wasn't until she butchered Dad's surname that we paused and turned around.

"It's pronounced *Ad-a-mal-e*," said Dad with a chuckle. It happened too often for him to get upset.

The receptionist blushed, then wiggled the phone in her hand. "Somebody's asking to speak to you."

Mum glanced at Sarah. "I left the hotel number with the hospital. It must be them."

Sarah reached out and grabbed Mum's arm like she might fall, while Dad took the phone from the red-lipped receptionist and placed it to his ear. "Hello, this is Mr Ademale."

A short conversation ensued that I couldn't decode, hearing only my dad's grunts and short replies. We were forced to wait until he put down the phone and faced us.

"What is it?" Sarah begged. "What is it?"

"The police. They've asked us to go back to the hospital immediately. That's all they would say."

For a moment, I assumed Courtney had died, but then I changed my mind and decided it would be something much worse.

I was right.

15

Sarah sobbed in the car, obviously assuming, as I first had, that Courtney was dead. I wondered if it might be true. His face had been mutilated, sure, but that wouldn't kill a person, right? Being blind and deaf wasn't fatal. The more I considered it, the more I decided the police hadn't called because Courtney had died. No, it was something else. Sarah had made a careless wish and now something bad would happen. That's what Thomas Quick had warned me about. As much as the stranger scared me, I desperately wanted to talk to him again. I wanted to talk with anyone who could explain what was happening to my family.

The previous night, Dad had sped us to the hospital with Courtney in the car, but that morning he drove sedately, almost like he was trying to put off arriving. We all knew that as soon as we entered the hospital the next part of our nightmare would begin, and so when Dad pulled up in the car park, I clutched my seatbelt for dear life.

"I don't want to go in," I said. "It's going to be bad."

Sarah sobbed.

"The police want to speak to us all," said Dad.

I shook my head. "I don't feel good. I want to stay in the car."

Mum reached back and held my knee. She couldn't look at me directly around the seat, but I saw the edges of her sympathetic smile. "Honey, it'll be okay. Let's just get it over with. Then we can do something fun afterwards."

"Like what?"

"I don't know. Bowling, perhaps."

I wasn't a massive fan of bowling, but at least it would delay us having to go back to the house. "Okay, fine, I'll come."

Dad smiled at me. "Thanks, buddy. Just let me do the talking and we'll be fine, okay?"

I unbuckled my seatbelt and got out of the car, slamming the door and marching ahead. Now that I had decided this was happening, I wanted to deal with it quickly. The anticipation of what came next was unbearable.

"Hold on, Martin," Dad shouted. "I don't want you wandering off by yourself."

I stopped and waited for them, but I tapped my foot to show my irritation. I wanted them to hurry up, and it was an eternity before we reached the hospital's front desk.

A nurse acknowledged us. "Ah, yes, Mr Ademale, we've been told to expect you. Officer Dorrens is waiting for you in the staff area. I'll have someone escort you."

Mum and Dad looked at each other. Probably a bad sign that the police were waiting for us in a private area of the hospital. They clearly had lots to talk about. Maybe they would arrest us as soon as we stepped into the room. A sting, or whatever they called it.

A man in a white uniform arrived to take us. He must have been from the same part of Africa as Dad's family, because they started chatting in Shona, the other language he knew besides English. The conversation ended with a laugh and the man patted Dad on the back.

Mum frowned. "Made a new friend?"

"He's from a village less than ten miles from where my parents grew up. Small world, huh?"

Sarah tutted. "Can we go find out about Courtney now, please?"

"Sure, sorry, come on."

We continued following the hospital employee as he led us through a corridor full of nurses who eyeballed us as we passed. Finally, he led us inside a room with a large table and chairs. A projector sat on top of the table but it wasn't switched on. PC Dorrens was sitting at the end, sorting through a stack of papers. He looked up and frowned when we entered. "Sit down, all of you. There are questions I want to ask."

"How is Courtney?" Sarah blurted. "Is he okay?"

The officer turned his paperwork face down and leant back in his chair. "That's why I asked you here. It appears some kind elaborate joke has been played that even the doctors can't make sense off. Now is the time to come clean before things get very serious."

Dad shook his head in confusion. "We have no idea what you're talking about. What joke?"

PC Dorrens sat forward and laced his fingers together on the desk. He seemed to study my dad for a moment. "Courtney has made a miraculous recovery. His eyes are fine. His hearing has returned. He's even spoken a little. It's as though Jesus himself walked in and healed him."

Sarah pulled out a chair and collapsed into it. I thought she would wail with relief, but she just stared at the wall in silence. Mum and Dad remained standing, but my legs ached, so I collapsed into the chair beside Sarah. I leaned into her and whispered, "You wished for this. You wished for Courtney to be okay."

She glanced at me, and from the way her eyes widened, I could tell she wasn't immediately dismissing my words. I had warned her not to make a wish, but she did so anyway. Now it had come true and there would be a price to pay. Thomas Quick had spoken of debts.

Mum folded her arms and slowly shook her head. "Courtney is really okay? How is that possible?"

"He was obviously fine to begin with," said PC Dorrens. "His wounds must have been prosthetics or make-up; nobody is quite sure. If he's practising to be a magician, he's well on his way to becoming a very good one. That doesn't mean he's going to get away with this. He's guilty of wasting hospital resources and police time. Christ, even his poor parents were duped. I stayed up half the night with them. His mother needed to be sedated. Whatever this is, it's sick and criminal. I want answers."

"We don't have any," said Dad. "I swear to you."

I flinched as the police officer suddenly turned his attention to me. "Answer me truthfully, Martin. You said you found Courtney at your front door. Was that a lie?"

I shook my head vigorously. "It's the truth. He was a mess, I swear. If this is all a joke, then Courtney played it on us too."

PC Dorrens turned to my sister next, but she continued staring at the wall. "I would ask *you*, Sarah, if you knew anything about this, but from the state you appear to be in, I would say not. Unless you're as a good an actress as Courtney is a magician."

Sarah turned her head just enough to look at the officer. "I don't understand what's happening."

PC Dorrens let out a grunt. "Ten years on the force and I've never seen anything like this. If any of you is involved, I promise you'll answer for it. Now, I can't question you kids alone, and quite frankly I don't want to. Mum and Dad, however, I will be interviewing you both separately, starting with you, Mr Ademale."

Mum and Dad glanced at each other. Were they thinking Courtney had actually tricked them? Or were they trying to figure out exactly how he had miraculously healed? I knew the answer even if they didn't.

The room granted wishes.

But not for free.

I wondered when our next payment was due.

16

Courtney's family didn't want us seeing him, but Sarah had been beside herself to a point that they eventually relented. They seemed like nice people. Younger than my own parents, they both had the same straight blonde hair as Courtney. They made small talk with my family for a while but eventually drifted to the other side of the waiting room. They seemed angry with us, but they didn't say so. They had gone through a nightmare only to have it revealed to be a false alarm. Their heads must have been a mess. Courtney's mum appeared half-asleep.

The nurse told us we couldn't see Courtney until the doctor confirmed it, which led to us waiting for nearly an hour. Then, when she finally gave us the okay, we were informed that only two of us were allowed in.

Dad waved a hand at Sarah. "You and Martin go."

Sarah rolled her eyes at me. "Can't he stay out here?"

I probably should have left Sarah alone with her boyfriend, but I was as upset about everything as she was. I needed to see Courtney too.

The nurse led us into a dimly lit room that smelled of bleach. Courtney was lying in a high bed, and when we entered he turned his head. His staring eyes sent a shudder down my neck. How had they healed? Had they just reappeared inside the sockets? Or had they grown back piece by piece, blood vessels kitting together like magic?

I didn't know what I'd expected, but Courtney didn't seem okay. 'Empty' was the word I would have used to describe him. He blinked and stared, blinked and stared, dreaming with his eyes open. His face lacked any expression – a doll's face.

Sarah galloped to the side of the bed and threw her arms around him. "Thank God you're okay. I'm so sorry this happened, but it's over now, babe. You're okay."

"S-Sarah?"

Sarah eased back. "Yes, I'm here for you, Courtney."

He nodded, but didn't smile. "I-I remember."

"Of course you do. Baby, I love you."

"Flesh screaming," he muttered, his voice weak. "Hooks in my eyes. Pulling me apart."

Sarah stepped away from the bed. "C-Courtney, what are you...?"

Courtney glanced in our direction, but it was like he barely knew we were there. "I counted the seconds," he said. "I counted them and they went on forever. The hooks took me away, chunk by chunk, until I was all gone. Now I'm back."

Sarah stepped forward again and grabbed Courtney by the arms. "Yes, you're back. Everything is okay, babe, I promise."

Courtney blinked rapidly as if his mind suddenly zapped back into his head. He then looked at Sarah and seemed to finally see her properly. "Why am I here?" he begged. "Why did I come back?"

"Babe... I..."

"You wished him back," I whispered to my sister, "but we have no idea where he was while he was gone. We don't know where the room took him."

"Shut up, Martin! Just shut up, you idiot."

Courtney shoved an arm out and almost hit Sarah in the face. "Why am I here?" he yelled. "Why did I come back? Why am I here? Why did I come back?" He kept saying the same thing over and over again, his voice increasing in volume until he was shouting at the top of his lungs.

Sarah went stiff as a board, barely moving at all. Courtney screamed right at her, his expression one of absolute madness. I worried he might hurt her.

"Sarah, get away from him." I reached out and grabbed her just as Courtney took a swing. He missed and tumbled out the bed, hitting the tiles hard, which caused Sarah to scream. She moved to help him, but I kept her back. Courtney thrashed on the ground, his teeth chomping at the air.

A nurse burst into the room behind us. "What is going on here?" She then saw Courtney on the ground and hurried over to help him. Grabbing him beneath the arms, she dragged him to his feet as if he weighed nothing at all. Once Courtney was upright, she placed a hand on his shoulder and looked him in the eye. "Everything is okay now, sweetie. Let's get you back into bed, shall we?"

Courtney blinked, over and over, then suddenly stopped. His head tilted and a smile grew on his face. If ever there was an expression of pure madness, this was it.

Nobody said anything, and I couldn't stand it.

"Courtney, please calm down," I said.

Courtney exploded into action, clawing at the nurse's face with both hands. The nurse screamed, first in shock, then in agony as he shoved his thumbs deep into her eyes. She collapsed to the ground, a wailing mess.

I'm not sure how I kept from being sick.

I reached out for my sister, wanting to get her away from the deranged monster that had once given me half a pack of Rolos, but she wouldn't come. She was a statue, only her eyes moving, which were fixated on Courtney.

Thankfully, he didn't move to hurt her. Instead, he turned to me, his eyes like those of a wild animal. I put my hands up, like I was being robbed by a gunman. "Please, don't hurt us, Courtney."

"L-Little man?"

I smiled with great effort, worried I was about to wet myself. "Yeah, it's little man, your friend. I want to help you."

Courtney shook his head. "No one can help me."

I flinched because I thought he was going to lunge at me, but his sudden movements sent him back towards the bed. He mumbled something, but I couldn't hear it because of the blinded nurse still wailing on the floor. She needed help badly.

Courtney gnashed his teeth again, snapping at the air like a dog catching flies. He raised both hands in front of himself, palms up like he was waiting to be handcuffed.

"Courtney, what are you—"

He bit down on his wrist like it was a chicken breast. Blood spurted into the air and drenched his face. He then bit into his other wrist and opened up a second artery. A shower of blood filled the room, the scent like tangy copper – the smell of death. My stomach turned, but not because I felt ill. It turned because I was seeing things no ten-year-old should ever see.

Sarah still didn't move, but she did scream. People started to file into the room behind us, but the shock of what they encountered meant they didn't approach further. Courtney was performing some sort of sick show and his growing audience was dumbstruck.

Courtney turned his back on us. He lifted both bleeding wrists over his head and pressed them against the wall. I thought maybe he was trying to stop them from bleeding, but then he started waving them back and forth.

Forming letters with his blood.

More people entered the room, and I spotted the man who had spoken to my dad earlier in Shona. He raced forward and tackled Courtney, throwing him onto the bed and restraining him. All this I witnessed in the corner of my eye because I was transfixed on the word Courtney had just spelled out on the wall in his own blood.

H-E-L-L.

Then Sarah and I were bundled out of the room and I saw nothing else. Thirty minutes later, a doctor came and spoke to us.

17

PC Dorrens was fuming. He was fuming at the hospital staff and he was fuming at us. His furious marching took him here, there, and everywhere, but he didn't seem to have an actual destination in mind. My family was sitting in the hospital's staffroom, watching him through the long windows. After a while, a man in a horrible brown jacket arrived and claimed to be a counsellor. He took me and my sister away and spent just short of an hour teaching us about emotional trauma and grief. We left his office with a collection of depressing leaflets, including one about suicide that Sarah read as we walked.

"You're not going to do anything stupid, are you?" I asked.

"No," was all she said in reply.

We re-entered the staffroom and found Dad talking to PC Dorrens. The officer was just leaving, and he gave us a terse smile before leaving without saying hello. I was glad. The last thing I wanted was more questions. My head was so full of them that any more would make my brain burst.

Mum was sitting in the corner of the room with her

head in her hands. Dad was standing and looked exhausted. I didn't even know what time it was, or even if it was sunny or dark outside. My tummy was rumbling, so I guessed it was dinnertime. We were definitely way past lunch.

Dad pinched the bridge of his nose and groaned. "Take a seat, kids. Your mum needs a few minutes, but then we'll go home."

Mum lifted her head and stared into space, just like she had done in the kitchen right before Keith had turned up on our doorstep. I could hardly believe that my birth father's sudden appearance was the least important thing going on in my life right now.

"Mum, are you okay?"

"Yes, honey, I'm fine." Her voice sounded right, but she didn't look at me.

I sat down on a comfy chair in the corner and reached for a magazine on the small table beside it. When I saw it was about wedding dresses, I changed my mind, and Sarah took it instead. It surprised me how well she was keeping herself together. She was quiet, and clearly upset, but she wasn't freaking out. Two hours ago, she had watched her boyfriend murder himself, yet somehow she was coping.

Or so I thought.

"What did PC Dorrens want?" I asked my dad.

"Answers I couldn't give him because I don't have any. Who can make any sense of this? You all knew Courtney better than me. Were there any warning signs that he might kill himself?"

"No," said Sarah. "He was normal. He was great."

Dad patted her knee and she allowed him to. "I'm really sorry about this, sweetheart. You're being really brave."

Sarah nodded. I noticed she was barely blinking.

"Has anyone seen his parents?" I asked. "Where did they go?"

Dad exhaled and put his hands on his hips. "A doctor came and took them away as soon as they got the news about Courtney. I was nearby when they found out. It was horrible. They're probably blaming themselves."

Sarah frowned. "Why would they do that?"

"That's what parents do. They'll be wondering if there was anything they did wrong."

The thought of Courtney's parents blaming themselves for this was unfair. It wasn't their fault, it was ours. Saying the truth out loud seemed nearly impossible, but I felt I had to. "The room in our house grants wishes. Sarah wished for Courtney to come back and he did. Then she wished for him to get better and his wounds vanished. Every time we make a wish, it comes true, but there are consequences. We have to pay the room for our debts."

Dad tutted. "Don't be ridiculous, Martin."

"I'm not. We've all seen the room. It appeared out of nowhere. It's evil."

"There's no such thing as evil, Martin."

"Yes, there is," said Sarah. "The room took Courtney from me."

"There's no room, kids. It's something we imagined, or... Christ, I don't know. We just need to think clearly. Fantasies aren't going to make anything better."

"The room grants wishes," I said again, defiantly. "Sarah, you believe me, don't you?"

She looked at me, her usually green eyes now washed out and grey. "I don't know."

Dad shook his head and started laughing. "You know what, Martin? It would be great if wishes came true. It's about time this family had a bit of luck. Hey, guess what I wish for?"

"Dad, don't!"

"I wish this family had a hundred thousand pounds. Come on! I wish to have lots of money, so where is it?"

I groaned. Even Sarah seemed dismayed.

The light bulb overhead flickered.

"You shouldn't have done that," I said. "You idiot!"

Dad flinched, shocked by my rudeness. "Martin!"

I stood and pointed at him. "No, you think you're being funny, but this isn't a joke. Courtney's dead because of us – because of the wishes we made. If I hadn't wanted a Big Mac he might still be here. If Sarah hadn't wished for..."

Sarah looked at me, but she didn't argue. She looked weak, broken, and even skinnier than usual. I hadn't seen her eat anything in the last two days, besides half a sausage. Maybe she wasn't coping after all.

"I've had enough of this," said Dad. "What has happened to this family? You've all gone mad."

"You're the only one who's mad," I said.

Mum exhaled loudly. "Martin, please calm down. You're getting carried away."

"No, I'm not. For once, I'm not getting carried away at all. Dad just made a wish and we're going to have to pay for it."

Dad stepped towards me. I didn't know his intentions, so I backed away. Charlie had never hit me before, but I supposed there was always a first time. Strangely, a memory of my real dad – Keith – popped into my head that made me shiver. I had spilled juice on his cigarettes so he was spanking me.

I had a feeling it wasn't the first time.

Dad grabbed me and pulled me into a great big hug. "It'll be okay, Martin. I won't let anything happen to this family, I promise. There's no such thing as wishes or evil or demon rooms. What we're dealing with here is a tragedy, and it's making things hard to understand. Can I tell you something my father told me when I was your age?"

I was trapped in his strong arms, so I couldn't exactly argue. I managed a shrug.

"Okay, this is something he told me when I lost my Aunt Moti. He said that grief is an ocean and family is a boat. Do you understand what that means?"

"That if we stick together, we'll be okay?"

He eased back so he could smile at me. "Yes, and eventually we'll reach the shore, where we can look back upon the ocean without fear; but if we step away from our family, we will drown in the ocean. We will drown in our grief."

"I want to go home," said Sarah.

I gawped at her. "You want to go back home? What about—"

"I just want to go home."

I shook my head. "We should never go back. We should never—"

"Martin," Dad interrupted, "we have to go home eventually. We can't live on the streets, and if I don't go to work tomorrow I'll get fired. We need to do everything we can to get back to our normal lives."

"I can't go back, Dad. I can't be normal after this."

He hugged me again. "I'm only asking you to try. We stick together and nothing can hurt us."

I nodded. Going home was the worst thing I could think of, but it also felt like the only thing. Like Dad said, where else could we go? It wasn't as if bad things weren't happening to us outside of the house. My life no longer seemed my own and things would happen whether I liked it or not.

Dad gathered Mum to her feet and held her by the hand. Sarah stood and started shuffling like a zombie. I walked beside her, bumping her now and then to keep her heading in the right direction. We stopped outside the hospital to pay for our parking, which made Dad hiss when it ate an entire ten-pound note. We headed for the car.

As I thought, it was past dinnertime, almost seven o'clock. I wanted to eat before going home, but when I considered broaching the subject, I decided I didn't want to cost Dad any more money. Hunger was something I would just have to deal with. At least it would give me nothing to throw up if I got sick again.

We walked up the hill in silence, heading for where we parked. Mum nestled her head into Dad, which cheered me up a little. Maybe we *would* get through this eventually.

"*Machende!*" We all stopped as Dad lifted his leg and looked down at the ground.

Mum frowned. "What's wrong, Charlie?"

"I stepped in chewing gum. Ah, never mind, what does it even matter? Just hold on a sec." He placed a hand on Mum's shoulder and reached down towards his shoe. As well as gum, there was a scrap of paper stuck to his sole. When he pulled it free, the pink gum stretched like intestines and made me grimace.

"Gross," said Sarah.

Dad pulled the scrap of paper free and examined it. It was actually a piece of colourful card with pictures of fruit all over it and gold lettering. I turned my head to read what it said.

JUNGLE CASH BONANZA.

"It's a scratch card," said Dad. "Why anyone wastes money on these things, I don't kn…"

My stomach told me something was wrong, and Dad's strange expression confirmed it. "What is it, Dad?"

"It's... It's a winner. Three bananas in a row. The jackpot."

For the first time in days, my mum seemed energetic and alive. "How much is it for?"

Dad moved the scratch card closer to his face, his eyes flicking left and right. The colour drained from his cheeks as he looked up at Mum. "A hundred grand."

Mum leaned to one side, and at first I thought she had a crick in her neck, but then she kept on going. Dad caught her just in time. "Whoa there! Do you need to sit down?"

"I can't... I can't believe it. Is it real?"

Dad kept her on her feet. "I don't know, so let's not get excited. Knowing our luck, it's somebody's idea of a practical joke."

"It's not a joke, Dad." I stood in front of him, in disbelief at his stupidity. Did he not see what this was? "You wished for a hundred thousand pounds and here it is, but I already told you it doesn't come for free. You don't know what you've done."

Dad looked at me and the smile wiped from his face. I think he finally understood the trouble we were in.

18

Daylight was waning by the time we got back to our house. The last time we'd been there, we had been in such a rush that we'd left the front door unlocked and half the lights on.

"It's lucky we didn't get burgled," said Dad, shaking his head in despair. "If Diane had known, she'd have nicked all the change from under our sofa cushions."

We all chuckled.

"Don't be horrible," said Mum. "She's had a hard life."

"Welcome to the club, Sharon," said Dad, but then he seemed to realise he was being grumpy. "Maybe you should go see her later."

I moved into the hallway and glanced up the stairs. I couldn't believe that we weren't talking about the only thing that mattered. "Are we going to see if it's still up there or what? We have to know."

Dad sighed. "I suppose we won't be able to get on until we do."

"I don't want to go up there," said Sarah. "I'll be in the living room. Just let me know."

I was disappointed she wouldn't be with us when we checked, but I was even more upset when Mum said she wasn't going either.

Dad patted me on the back. "Looks like it's just us men. You ready?"

I nodded. As terrifying as things were, I was eager to get upstairs and see if the door was still there. It was an evil thing, yes, but I felt like its main power lay in the fact that we didn't understand it. Maybe if we took our time and stood our ground, we would learn what it was.

And how to make it go away.

Dad positioned me behind him on the stairs and we headed up. Every step creaked. My bladder fizzed. My stomach sloshed. There was something invisible in the air. I couldn't see it, but I could *feel* it.

Dad stepped onto the landing first. I tried to see around him but couldn't. "Is it there?" I asked. "Is it?"

He turned to me and smiled. "No. There's nothing here."

I stepped around him and saw the blank wall at the end of the landing. The door was gone, but I wasn't willing to trust my eyes.

"What are you doing, Martin?"

"I need to see. I need to know it's really not here."

Dad's belief in the room was less than mine, but I heard the nervousness in his voice. "Be careful."

"You want us to get back to normal, right? Then I need to know for sure." I moved slowly, like the way a hunter most probably approached a deer. The door might have been hiding, playing games. It had disappeared before, and it had come back. I reached out a hand and I could swear I felt something. The splinter in my thumb throbbed, the tips of my fingers tingled, but when I pressed my hand against the wall everything felt normal. Nothing but smooth old paint. "It's really not here," I said. "Do you think it'll come back?"

"No," said Dad, so quickly that he couldn't have given it any thought. "Everything is fine now, I promise."

"You can't promise that."

"I can. Things are going to get better now, okay?"

"What are you going to do with the scratch card?" I asked.

"I don't know. If it's real, then I think we have to cash it in. It's a hundred thousand pounds, Martin. We can't ignore money like that."

"Maybe you're right, but—"

Our bathroom toilet flushed.

Dad and I looked at each other, our eyebrows raised curiously. Sarah and Mum were downstairs, so who the heck was in our bathroom? Dad put his finger against his lips and moved to the side of the bathroom door. I moved down the landing, out of direct sight.

The bathroom door opened. Someone stepped out. Dad grabbed the intruder by the scruff of the neck and swung them out onto the landing. He raised his fist to throw a punch, but stopped himself. "Mike? What on earth are you doing here?"

Mike held his hands up, shielding his face. "Whoa! Don't hurt me."

I stood in front of my best friend, glad to see him but also shocked. "What are you doing here, mate?"

Mike was taller than me, and better looking too. His black hair formed curtains either side of his thick eyebrows that the girls in our year seemed to love. He was popular and cool, but I was his best mate, which meant I was popular and cool too. Seeing him now made me feel like everything might be okay. It still didn't explain what he was doing in our house though.

Mike shrugged. "I ain't seen you since last week, geeza. I came by to see if you were okay, but no one answered. Door was unlocked, so thought I'd come check if you were sleeping off a dodgy belly or summin'. You weren't here though, so I was about to go, but nature called. I didn't mean to break in or nuffin'."

Dad patted Mike on the arm. "I didn't mean to give you a scare, Mike. You're always welcome here, but I'm not sure Martin wants company right now. It's been a difficult few days."

"Oh, right. Fair enough."

It was true, of course, but I couldn't deny how much better I felt seeing my friend. "Actually, Dad. I'd really like it if Mike could hang out for a bit."

Dad gave me a look, and I knew he was warning me not to tell Mike about things he wouldn't understand. I gave a tiny nod, letting him know I understood. The last thing I intended was to make my best friend think I was crazy.

Dad sighed. "It's getting late. I'll fix you something to eat, but then Mike will have to go home."

I nodded and led Mike into my room. He took up his usual position on the beanbag that I kept under my window. I sat on my bed crossed-legged.

"Come on then, mate, what's going on? Where've you been?"

My mouth opened but no sound came out. Where should I start? What could I tell him? And what must I never tell him?

"A lot's happened," I said simply, and then it all came spilling out. "Sarah's boyfriend was in an accident and he died at the hospital today."

Mike's eyes went wide. "You're joking?"

"I ain't. It's been a right horrible couple of days. He was a nice lad."

"Courtney, right? Yeah, I know him. He used to go out with my cousin, Sam."

"Really? I didn't know you knew him."

Mike shrugged. "I know everyone, mate. Anyway, it sucks to hear he's dead – although he did cheat on my cousin. Maybe it was karma."

I winced. Dad always told me to never speak ill of the dead, but it was more than just that. Whatever Courtney might have done in the past, he had been nice to me. I didn't want to think bad things about him.

"So, how did he die?" asked Mike, eyes sparkling in a way that made me want to reach out and thump him. This wasn't some ghost story like Annie May and the dump.

"He was... It... I'm not really sure. I'm just trying to be there for Sarah. She said she loved him."

Mike shifted on my beanbag, lifting one of his clearly brand-new trainers onto his knee. "Like 'em? Old man got another cheque for his worker's comp. Cost seventy quid."

I feigned happiness. The thing I disliked most about my best friend was how he always shoved his new stuff in my face. Surely he must have known my family struggled with money, but he didn't seem to care. Did he like upsetting me? "Speaking of dads," I said, "my real dad turned up on our doorstep the other day. That's the other thing my family has been dealing with."

"No way! That's cool, man. Two dads means twice the presents on birthdays and Christmas. Jammy bastard."

"Mike, the last thing I've been thinking about is how many presents I'm gonna get at Christmas. My real dad abandoned me. I don't know if I even want to see him."

Mike put his leg down and leant forward. His smirk went away and he nodded. "Sorry, mate. Can I do anything?"

"Just help take my mind off it."

"No problem." He hopped up from the bean bag and put his hands on his hips. "You free tomorrow?"

"I think so."

"Cool. Then we're gonna hang out and have a laugh. I'll bring my N64 round."

That was music to my ears. "Thanks, man. It means a lot."

"Hey, it's no problem. You're my best mate. My job is to cheer you up when you're sad."

I smiled. "I think you should probably go home for now though. My family's pretty stressed out."

"I'll bet. Okay, just let me take a slash and I'll get out of your hair, mate."

"You need to go again? Jesus, you literally just came out of our bathroom five minutes ago."

"I know, right? I had a large bottle of *Lucozade* on the walk over here. If I don't go now, I'll end up going in the bushes by the bumpy slide. Hey, maybe we should hang out there tomorrow. Tracy Collins lives right behind it. Maybe we'll see her."

I smirked. Tracy Collins was a good enough reason to do anything. "Sounds like a plan."

"Sorted."

I remained cross-legged on my bed while Mike went the toilet. My Karazy Klown doll was lying on its side next to my TV. I was surprised Mike hadn't seen it, and I considered showing it to him, knowing he'd be jealous. He got nearly everything he asked for, but his mum was strict about horror movies and other adult stuff. Even with all of his dad's compensation money, Mike would never be allowed a Karazy Klown. But showing him would just make him feel as rotten as I did whenever he flashed his latest pair of trainers at me. I left the doll where it was.

Mike should've finished taking a whizz by then, but it didn't sound as if he'd even started. What was he doing in there?

"Mike? You finished or what?"

He didn't answer.

I got off the bed and crossed my room. I wasn't in the habit of following my friends to the toilet, but I wanted to make sure he hadn't bumped into Sarah or said anything to upset my parents. Mike had a way of getting me into trouble.

On the landing, I looked towards the bathroom. The door was open. No one was inside. I could see the toilet and the seat was down.

"Hey, Martin."

The sound of Mike's voice was a relief, and I turned to face the direction it had come from, further along the landing. I spotted him and he had a massive grin on his face.

He was standing inside the room.

My knees deserted me and I slumped against the wall, bashing my elbow and hurting myself. I didn't care about the pain; I cared about my best friend. "Mike... no..."

He was still beaming, the happiest I'd ever seen him. "I don't get it," he said. "How did you build an extension? Where did you get the money?"

The room wasn't empty like it had been before. This time it was full. A pinball machine stood directly behind Mike and a pool table filled the room to his left.

My mouth was dry. It was hard to speak. "M-Mike, you need to get out of there."

"You have a frikkin' games room, mate. How could you keep this a secret?"

Tears filled my eyes, blurred my vision. "Mike, please just come out of there. It's... It's not safe."

Mike frowned. "What d'you mean, it's not safe? Is it not finished or something? It looks finished to me. There's a *Mortal Kombat* machine in here. My mum would freak. Come on, Martin. Let's play a couple of rounds. Then I'll go, yeah?"

I didn't see a *Mortal Kombat* machine inside the room, and the pinball machine and pool table began to shimmer before my eyes. They weren't real. They were tricks.

Bait.

I raised my voice, sheer panic working its way through my lungs. "Mike! Get the fuck out of there, right now!"

Mike flinched. I don't think he'd ever heard me use the F-word before. Or shout it. He held his palms up to me and frowned. "Yeah, okay, Martin. What's your problem?"

Mike took a step towards me and my breath caught in my throat. Perhaps he would just walk out of the room and everything would be fine. He just had to keep moving until he was safely back on the landing.

Mike paused. A puzzled expression crossed his face. One of his hands rose above his head, the fingers pointing straight out and quivering.

"Mike? What are you doing?"

He shook his head at me and I saw his confused expression turn to fear. His fingers kept on quivering as he held them up above his head.

Snap!

Mike's index finger bent backwards at the knuckle, a twig broken in two. The sound it made was like a gunshot. His screams were like a siren blaring.

Snap! Snap!

Two more of his fingers snapped backwards. His screaming stopped. His throat bulged like he was trying to bring up an apple.

His entire arm snapped at the elbow.

Mike looked like a puppet on tangled strings. He managed to look at me, his eyes blotted with tears and blood. "M-Martin?"

Crack!

Mike's neck twisted a full three-hundred-and-sixty degrees, his face turning a full circle. His eyes bulged in their sockets. His neck was a coil of old rope.

And just like that, my best friend was gone.

A hand grabbed me. I shrieked, but then saw it belonged to Dad. Mum and Sarah were standing with him, and all three of them were staring into the room – staring at Martin's suspended body. Apparently, the room wasn't done with him yet. The flesh beneath his eyes and around his thick black eyebrows twitched. It looked like invisible crows were pecking at his face one moment and invisible hooks tugging at his skin the next.

"Dad?" I didn't know what else to say. Nor did Dad, because all he did was squeeze my arm tighter.

There was a sudden *whoosh* and Mike's face was ripped away from his skull. Then, like a sheet being pulled from a table, his flesh was torn from his body and he stopped being even a memory of friend. He was an anatomical dummy – muscles, flesh, and veins.

The room's door slammed shut.

I collapsed backwards into Dad's arm.

Sarah started screaming. I think I did too.

PART III

19

W e tumbled downstairs, all of us screaming. If we needed any more convincing to shatter our spirits completely, it had been offered in spades. Something evil was inside our house and it fed on innocent flesh. First Courtney, now Mike.

My best friend.

"We need to call the police," said Sarah. "I don't want to do this any more. I'm done. I'm done. I'm done."

"Just move." Dad shoved her in the back. "We need to get out of here."

"What if we can't leave?" I fretted. "Like last time. What if it doesn't let us leave?"

"We'll cross that bridge when we come to it, Martin."

In the hallway we wasted no time, moving in a panicked jumble towards the door. "Get straight to the car," said Dad. "I'm driving us to the police station. We can't hide from this any more."

I was at the front of the pack, so it was me who yanked open the front door, jabbering and half-mad with relief when it opened.

A man stood on our doorstep, the night behind him. Someone I instantly recognised. Beneath his baseball cap, Thomas Quick's expression was grim. He seemed unsurprised to see my family attempting to flee the house. "Whatever you're all planning to do," he said calmly, "I suggest you don't. Invite me in. We need to talk."

"Who the hell are you?" Dad demanded, his fists rising slightly in front of him.

Mr Quick glanced at me and smiled. "I'm a friend of Martin's. The boy's been expecting me."

It was true. I had been hoping to see this bizarre stranger again. "You can really help us?" I asked him.

"I can really try."

Dad blocked the doorway with his arm. "Who the hell are you and what do you know about my family?"

Quick lowered his head and his shoulders, almost like he was bowing. "Your lives have been taken over by evil – an evil that needs to be fed. Invite me in, Mr Ademale, and allow me to aid you."

I turned to Dad and tugged at his arm to get his attention. When he failed to stop staring at the man on our doorstep, I had to urge him to listen. "We need help. He knows what's going on."

Mr Quick gave me a friendly smile, revealing several golden teeth. "I would also add, what do you folks have to lose?"

Dad glared, looking like he might grab the man and fight him, but he moved away from the door and grunted. "Fine, but if you try to hurt my family, I'll kill you."

"Fair enough," said Quick, who then stepped into our hallway like a fox entering a henhouse. He took off his leather jacket and draped it on our bannister. "Any tea going?"

Dad spluttered at the request, but Mum headed towards the kitchen without complaint. "How do you take it?"

Quick grinned, flashing those gold teeth again. "Milk and a whole lot of sugar, please, ma'am."

"Let's go into the living room," I said, and surprisingly everyone did. After seeing Mike get torn apart, I no longer cared about being a quiet, polite child. I wanted to know about the evil that had invaded our house – and how to kill it.

We waited for Quick to start talking, but he sat in silence until my mum arrived with his cup of tea. He sipped at it and then smacked his lips. "Ambrosia. Thank you for that."

Dad was bouncing his knee and fidgeting. "Can you get on with what you came here to say? You said you can help us. Do you know what's going on?"

Quick put his tea down on the coffee table carefully, making sure it fit perfectly on the coaster. "I know fully what is happening to your family, yes. As I told your boy, you folks have brought something into your home. I'm sorry I couldn't help sooner, but these things need to be dealt with cautiously."

Dad shook his head and didn't look like he was buying it. "What exactly do you think we've brought into our home?"

Quick shrugged. "You'd know better than me. Djall can take on any form it wishes, but once a person covets it, they give up their souls to its hunger."

"What's a Djall?" I asked.

"Not *a* Djall, just Djall. I suppose you could call it a demon. This particular demon feeds on misery. It grows strong on agony. Like most demons, there is no rhyme nor reason to why it does what it does. It is just what it is. Evil rarely considers being anything else other than evil."

Dad pinched the bridge of his nose and let his head sag. "Demons? You're telling us that we have a demon in our home? This is..." He shook his head and laughed. "I want to say ridiculous, but I think we're past that."

"So this demon is called Dal?" Mum asked. I was glad to see her taking it seriously, because everything told me to trust this man, Quick. If it turned out that he couldn't help us, I didn't see what else could.

Quick laced his fingers together over his knees, every knuckle crisscrossed with scars. "Not Dal, Djall. It escape our possession about eighteen months ago. We've been monitoring the news, local police reports, and, more importantly, hospital cases. When we were alerted to a patient who had been badly mutilated, blinded and made deaf, I came to investigate. That amount of suffering stunk of Djall. It's quite fond of blinding its prey before feeding."

Dad ran a hand over his bald head and sat up straight. "You said *we* were alerted. Who is *we*?"

"The Sphere," I answered, remembering that part of it from my earlier conversation with Quick. "They're an organisation."

Quick nodded at me appreciatively. "Yes, Martin. The Sphere of Zosimus. As I told you, our founder was a pagan from Roman times. It was he who first started to confront and contain the evils of this world. His occult writings serve as the credo for our organisation. We are dedicated to combatting the malevolent forces of this world and allowing innocent people to sleep at night."

Mum tittered. "You mean you fight demons?"

Quick flashed those gold teeth of his. "Just that, yes, and I have come to believe that Djall is inside this house. For hundreds of years he was stored in the Sphere's vaults, but two years ago we had an incident – a betrayal to be more precise. Members of our organisation are called caretakers, and only caretakers may enter the vaults. One of our members, Calendo Graves, unfortunately lacked the morals required to perform his duties. It sickens me to say, but he stole several of our wards in order to sell to the highest bidder. We found him dead at the side of the road in one of our vans, but all of the stolen relics were gone. I have been seeking Djall for more than a year now, knowing that I would not come close until someone suffered terribly. I'm afraid that someone is your family."

"And Courtney," said Sarah, not looking at any of us, or even really joining in the conversation. She was only half listening by the look of it.

"I heard about his passing," said Quick, "but it was probably for the best. That poor boy experienced agony and pain that I pray none of you ever has to endure."

"My friend is dead too." I pictured Mike's skin being pulled from his broken body. "The room took him. That's why we were leaving."

"My condolences. Did anybody know the boy was here?"

I shrugged. "I don't know."

"Well, let's hope not. The last thing we need is more people turning up while we do what needs doing."

A cloud lifted and I finally saw a light ahead. "And what needs doing? How do we stop this?"

"Firstly, we need to find out what form Djall took when you brought him into your home. It could have been an old book or an item of clothing. Quite often, Djall likes to hide in plain sight as a piece of jewellery. Does any of that ring a bell?"

I turned my head until I was looking at Sarah. She was staring down at the floor, but gradually she raised her face to look at us. She was still wearing the green glass necklace against her chest, but she grabbed at it and ripped it free, tossing it into the middle of the room. It lay there on the carpet, capturing light from a nearby lamp. "Oh my God, oh my God. I did this. I did this to us all? It was my necklace the entire time?"

Quick was a scar-covered monster, but the way he looked at my sister was all kindness. "None of this is your fault, girl. Evil doesn't target evil. It targets innocence and youth. It targets the best of us. You are not a facilitator of tragedy, only a victim. As are you all. I'm sorry Djall was ever allowed to escaped our possession. If you want to blame anyone, you can blame me, but there'll be time for that later. Now is the time to deal with this vile thing before us."

I stared at the beautiful, ancient, wicked necklace on our living room floor. Was it really evil? A demon? "How do we deal with it?"

Quick shrugged. "A little of this, a little of that. A ritual of sorts, for which you must all be present. Djall's wickedness extends to the accursed and their immediate family – a household. Some used to call Djall the 'Emerald Cuckoo' because it makes its home in the nest of others. Emerald because of the treasures it seemingly offers."

"It grants wishes," said Dad, and I was surprised to hear him admit it out loud. Whatever doubts he had been holding onto had obviously gone. He believed. Only Mum seemed doubtful. She followed along with the conversation, but it was like she wasn't really listening. Sarah was barely listening at all, but I knew she understood. She was broken, and I didn't know if she would ever recover.

Quick reached into his jeans pocket and pulled out a small notebook. Various pages were stuffed with scraps of other papers, and one of these scraps was a newspaper article, which he unfolded before our eyes. "We managed to locate and contain Djall in February 1808," he explained. "It fell into the hands of a London doctor named Daniel Jarvis, who specialised in maternity. Back then, baby deaths were unfortunately common. Doctor Jarvis, however, never lost a single child between the dates of March 1807 and January 1808. More and more expectant mothers passed through his care, and he became renowned in the city to a point that high society was willing to pay him a small fortune to deliver its babies. At the same time, a spate of disappearances plagued the city – vagrants, mostly, and the odd prostitute. These were people local enforcement cared little for, but it didn't escape the scrutiny of the Sphere. We have people whose entire job it is to look out for patterns and coincidences that escape the notice of others. Their investigations soon brought to light that Doctor Jarvis was preying on the vulnerable by night and making them all but vanish. He was feeding people to Djall in exchange for medical perfection."

"He was a monster," I said, wondering how someone could do such a thing, but Quick frowned at me as if he didn't agree,

"Possibly. Possibly not. You see, once Djall has a hold over a person, it will feed one way or another. If you refuse to feed it, it will feed on you. You'll start getting ill. Nosebleeds and tummy aches at first, just minor things, but if you continue to refuse Djall, he will strike you with festering boils and poisoning of the blood, feeding on you until there's barely anything left. Then you'll die. That's what happened to the person who possessed Djall before you. For whatever reason, a young man took possession of it six months ago and refused to feed it. The coroner said he died of a rapid cancer, but the truth is that he was such a withered mess that no one could really tell. We were unable to identify Djall from the young man's belongings, but we believe it was taken by a relative. Then it ended up in your hands."

"We got it at a car boot," I said, shaking my head and laughing at the absurdity of it all.

Mum alerted us with a sudden sob. Tears had come to her eyes. "My baby. My poor baby."

Dad sighed. "It's okay, Sharon, we'll get through this." He turned to Quick and spoke quietly. "Martin and Sarah have been getting ill. Nosebleeds, stomach aches, just like you said."

Quick looked my dad in the eyes. "To be expected. While Djall can only feed beneath the cover of the moon, its sickening influence is ever-present."

"The room has only appeared at night," I said. "That's why it's been coming and going?"

Quick nodded. "Evil does not like the light."

"My baby," Mum said again. She was shaking her head and weeping. "My baby."

I reached out a hand to her. "Mum, it's okay."

She looked at me with agony written across her face. "No, it's not. I made a wish and it came true. It came true."

My throat itched. I had to cough, but I suppressed it. "What did you wish for Mum?"

"I wished for it to be gone. We couldn't afford it and I wasn't even sure I wanted it. I wasn't sure until after it was gone."

Dad left his armchair and perched beside Mum on the sofa. "Sweetheart, what are you saying?"

She turned her head quickly to look at him. "I was pregnant, Charlie. I was eight weeks pregnant."

Dad opened his mouth, but nothing came out.

Mum saw that he needed more, so she continued.

"We've been struggling so much with money, and you work so much as it is... I wanted to tell you but I felt ashamed, like a goddamn teenager who forgot to take her pill."

Charlie moved away, and I thought he was angry, but then he readjusted his arm and gave Mum an even tighter hug. "You silly woman. I would've been over the moon. I love Martin and Sarah – you know that – but there's always room for more. Money isn't everything."

Mum wiped tears and snot from her face and grunted. "Well, it doesn't matter now, because on the night this all started, I went round Diane's to have a drink. I told her everything..." She started crying again. "I said I wished I wasn't pregnant. And now I'm not."

Dad shook his head. "Sharon, how do you know for sure? Have you seen a doctor?"

"I know because I don't feel it any more. My morning sickness, the tummy flutters. It's all gone. I've even lost three pounds."

"We haven't been eating."

"Charlie, I lost our baby. I'm telling you, I wished it away."

Quick let out a breath that captured everyone's attention. "I'm afraid that if you made the wish after bringing Djall into your lives, then what you say is most likely true. I'm sorry."

I didn't know how to feel. Mum had been pregnant and none of us knew it. Should that hurt? Because it did. I could have had a little brother or, God forbid, a little sister, but she had wished it away.

But I had made careless wishes too.

"You could never have known, Mum," I said. "It's not your fault."

She looked at me through tears. "I should never have wished such a thing."

"Wishes aren't supposed to come true," said Quick. "They're not meant to have power. That is the evil of Djall. I don't know what you're feeling, ma'am, but I am here to make sure that no more evil befalls this family."

Dad scowled at Quick, looking him up and down. "What are you? Some kind of soldier? It looks like you've been in a dozen wars."

Quick huffed and stared down at his scarred hands. "I wish the number were so low. I am a soldier, as you say, yes. I've spent my entire life waging war on the things that cause misery and pain without remorse. I pray I can help you folks find your way back into the light."

I saw my sister flinch, and when I stared at her, her nose was bleeding. She did nothing to stop it and allowed the blood to drip-drip-drip onto the carpet.

My stomach sickened, suddenly awash with burning liquids. "I feel ill," I said, but I didn't panic. "It's Djall, isn't it?"

Quick glared at the necklace in the middle of the room. "We should get started. Are you all ready?"

None of us were. But none of us had any choice.

20

Sarah's nose was bleeding worse than ever. Blood leaked from her face like she was melting, and she had to gasp like a goldfish to breathe. Mum rubbed her back while Dad tried to stem the blood with towels, but it only seemed to increase. I had thrown up twice in the last ten minutes, but I was too used to it now to let it keep me down. All I felt now was anger. I wanted to destroy the evil thing that was tormenting my family and had killed my friend. The thing that had taken away my baby brother or sister. The thing that had taken Courtney and Mike. I wanted to face it down and tear out its eyes or whatever it had for a face. I was ready to kill.

Quick stood in the corner of our living room, arms folded. He wasn't impatient, just still. It was like he had shut down, waiting until we were ready. I didn't even know if he would respond when I spoke to him, but he did. "Do you think Djall is scared that you're here?"

"A thing like Djall does not feel fear, boy, but like anything alive, it has a sense of self-preservation. It knows me well and, while it might not fear me, it knows why I'm here."

I looked up at this towering warrior and struggled to see the world in a new way. "Is there really a whole secret group of people like you, fighting monsters?"

"The world is full of monsters, from corrupt politicians to vampires. Many groups exist to tackle them, but the problem is that the monsters outnumber us by an insurmountable number. It's a war we can never win. We can only hold the line."

I didn't truly understand, but it sounded like the world was a worse place than I could ever have imagined. Would it one day end? Overrun by monsters? Devoured by demons? No, not if there were men like Quick in the world. He wasn't afraid. In fact, I couldn't picture him being afraid of anything. "How do we help my sister? There's so much blood. I'm worried."

"We help her by dealing with Djall. It can afford to take one of you as a warning, and I fear Sarah's suffering might be that warning. Djall is going to kill her if we don't act fast."

My stomach tried to purge itself again, but I fought it. I fought it and looked at my sister, stooped on the floor with blood gushing from her face. There was also a sore-looking blister spreading on her chin. Was she truly dying in front of me? "Sarah, I love you."

She looked up at me, shuffled across the carpet, then threw her arms around my waist. I lowered myself and the two of us embraced. This was a nightmare, and we were in it together.

Brother and sister.

"We need to move," said Quick. "Boy, hand me the necklace."

No one had disturbed the green gemstone in the centre of the room, and I looked at it now with disgust. As much as I hated Djall, I feared touching it.

Quick seemed to detect my displeasure. He waved a hand. "The necklace isn't actually Djall itself. It's just a totem, an object of power to which it is tethered. Pick it up now and give it to me."

Sarah let go of me, leaving me free to move. I reached down, my fingers hovering for a moment before finally picking up the piece of jewellery that had caught my sister's eye in what seemed like a lifetime ago. It seemed to vibrate in my palm, and I quickly thrust it into Quick's waiting hands. The tall man glared at it, his eyes narrowing to a point where they were almost closed.

Dad resumed trying to stem Sarah's bleeding nose with towels, but he looked at Quick as he did so. "What do we need to do?"

"We need to face Djall directly," said Quick. "You said it's been appearing as a room upstairs? Take me there."

We all shared a look. Being downstairs in the lounge had given us the illusion of safety. Going upstairs onto the landing felt like stepping into a lion's den. But running away was no option.

I moved to the door. "Come on. Let's get it over with."

Quick nodded at me and made me feel like an adult. "Charlie, gather your family and join us."

Dad didn't seem so sure any more, but he nodded silently and reached down to help Sarah up off the ground.

I found myself leading Quick upstairs by myself, a child leading a warrior. I took each step slowly, the creaking of the boards like ominous warnings. I reached the landing, hoping that the room would not be there, but I was given no comfort. The door at the end of the landing was closed, but it creaked as it slowly it fell open.

Nothing but darkness lay inside.

"Huh, I've never known Djall to take the form of a room," said Quick. "Once it appeared as a tailor's dummy, whispering wicked temptations to its owner, and another time it appeared as a painting, its depiction of an empty field changing constantly to show vile depictions of people being sacrificed upon alters. Never a room though."

I swallowed. "It tempted my friend to go inside by showing him arcade games and a pool table."

Quick put a large hand on my back, and its coldness made me shiver. "You're a strong boy, Martin. This is grown-up's work, but you're holding it together better than most men would. People usually look away from the universe's underbelly, but you face it with fascination and determination. The world could use more like you."

I felt my cheeks grow hot. "Thank you."

"No need to thank me for an observation."

My family came up the stairs behind us and we all gathered on the landing. Sarah's nose was still bleeding, her forehead glistening with sweat. The blister on her chin had now spread to the middle of her cheek. She slumped against the wall, barely conscious. Mum wasn't much better, but her weakness appeared more mental than physical. Her expression was... vacant.

Dad stepped up beside Quick and me. "It's still here."

Quick nodded, eyes fixed on the darkness of the room at the end of the landing. "Did you expect it not to be?"

"No. I just hoped for it."

"That's good. Hope isn't a useless thing, Charlie. Right now, it's the strongest weapon we have."

I looked up at Quick. "What happens now?"

He held up the necklace in his fist, its steel chain wrapped between his fingers. "Now we perform an eviction."

"Don't you mean an exorcism?" said Dad.

"I'm no priest. You have an unwanted guest and I intend to help you evict it."

It was clear that Quick was ready to take the lead, so we remained where we were on the landing while he approached the open doorway that shouldn't have been there. He thrust out the necklace and roared. "Djall, you have been found out. Your tricks and deceptions are to end. I possess your totem and command you to obey."

I shared a look with my dad, and I wondered if he was thinking what I was thinking – that more than simple words would be required to end this nightmare. Yet, words were all that Quick offered. He shouted and threatened, and commanded the demon to obey. Nothing seemed to happen though.

Then everything happened at once.

The door at the end of the landing slammed shut, then opened again, then slammed shut. It created an awful banging sound that made me cover my ears. Then the banging suddenly ceased and the door remained open. The darkness inside the room came alive, creating shadows that were like rolling black oil. Each wave of darkness released a chorus of screams, increasing in volume until it was impossible to even think. A howling wind of agony.

"It's terrible," I said, clutching at my ears. "What's happening?"

Quick kept looking ahead but put out a hand and probed the air until he caught my shoulder. "This is for my benefit, boy. Djall and I go back a ways. He knows things about me I would sooner forget."

I stared at the swirling black depths of the doorway and saw faces – pained faces crying out in agony. If this was for Quick's benefit, I had no understanding of what it meant.

"Your parlour tricks have no effect on me, Djall. You may know me, but I also know you. I know your power is built on quicksand. Harm this family if you will, but you will not find another after. You are going back into the vaults, and this time you shall stay there forever."

A blast of heat shot out of the room and forced us all to turn away. Sarah slid down the wall and collapsed onto the carpet. She was now soaked in her own blood and covered in blisters. A gurgling moan escaped her lips, and her eyes rolled back in her head. It forced Mum to snap out of her daze. She dropped to her knees and screamed, "Sarah! Sarah, wake up!"

Dad grabbed Quick. "What's happening to her?"

I looked at my sister and was in no doubt about the answer. "She's dying. Djall is killing her."

"Stay strong," Quick bellowed. "It's threatening us because it knows I'm here to end its games."

Dad looked at the man like he was an idiot, like he had lost faith in Quick as rapidly as he had found it. "You're doing nothing! You're telling this thing off like it's a naughty child."

"It's the only language Djall understands."

"Then why isn't it working?"

I saw a lump in Quick's throat as he swallowed, and the man seemed to deflate. "I don't know. Possessing the totem and demanding Djall to obey should be enough."

Dad snarled. "Are you fucking joking me? You think it's going to behave just because you tell it to?"

Quick turned on my dad with the speed of a hawk snatching a mouse, and before anyone could react, he had him up against the wall. "If you know a demon's true name and possess the totem that tethers it to this world, it must do your bidding. So it has been since the moment mankind oozed into existence. Something is wrong. We need to refocus and replan."

Sarah moaned from the floor. "D-Dad."

Dad pushed back against Quick, showing a violent streak I'd never seen before. "She doesn't have that long. I never should have invited you in."

I objected. "Sarah would be in trouble even if you hadn't. Dad, we were in trouble the moment she spotted the necklace at the car boot."

Dad released Quick, although it seemed like the tall man could have broken free at any point, and looked down at Sarah. "How do we stop it? How do we help her?"

"You cannot help her. Unless you're willing to surrender yourselves to Djall's bidding and do great evil, the only way to save Sarah is to command Djall to stop. But that isn't working."

Mum was shaking my sister on the ground, trying desperately to keep her from passing out. "Please, don't go. I can't lose you too."

"Hello? Hello, Sharon, are you home?"

Quick moved like a bird again, swooping to the top of the stairs. He looked at me and hissed. "Who is that?"

"I-It sounds like Diane, our neighbour," I said, and sure enough that was exactly who appeared halfway up our stairs. She looked surprised to see us all gathered there, but we were the more surprised, which was why nobody said anything to stop her joining. Before we knew it, she was standing on the landing.

"Oh, Sharon, whatever is the matter? Is... Is Sarah okay?"

For a moment, Mum didn't seem to recognise her best friend, but then she turned, as confused as the rest of us. "Diane? What are you doing here?"

"I just wanted to borrow some money so I can go get a bottle of sherry. Did you fancy popping round for an hour? I wanted to talk to you about something."

Mum blinked slowly. "W-What time is it?"

"Half past nine. The shop closes in half an hour so I need to go now. Can you lend me a few quid?"

Mum stood up and brushed herself off after lowering Sarah slowly to the carpet. She stood in front of Diane and frowned. "Sarah's sick? Do you not see that? Can you not keep yourself from scrounging for one minute and think about somebody else?"

Diane flinched, and I honestly didn't know how the words surprised her. In fact, I didn't know why Mum hadn't spoken them sooner. "Sharon, what has got into you? I really think you should come next door and we can have a proper talk. If we both leave now, we can catch the shop before it closes."

Sarah moaned. "M-Mum? What's happening?"

"Nothing sweetie. You're going to be just fine." Mum moved in front of Diane. "You selfish, drunken bitch." She grabbed Diane by her frizzy brown hair and yanked her forward, almost tossing her to the ground. She then proceeded to drag Diane across the landing.

Right towards the room.

"Mum, what are you doing?"

Dad reached out a hand but seemed rooted to the spot. He was unable to grab her. "Sharon, what are you doing?"

Diane screeched like a caught cat, and I couldn't believe the way my mum was manhandling her. She was more like a demon than Djall, a scowling monster. "Here, you're hungry? Take this bitch. Take her and leave my daughter alone. I'll feed you as much as you want. Just leave my family alone."

It's hard for a ten-year-old to understand many things, but watching my mum throw our neighbour into a room that was actually some kind of ancient monster was more than my brain could compute. My arms hung at my sides and my mouth fell open as I stood there in a stupor. I could do nothing but watch.

Diane twisted and tried to slip away as Mum gave her one last hard shove and sent her spiralling into the room. Her legs got tangled up and she fell to the ground. Her trouser legs rode up at the knees and I saw just how skinny Diane was. She was ill. I wondered if that was what booze had done to her.

Dad was still rooted to the spot, as shocked as I was to see Mum do what she was doing. "Sharon, you can't."

Mum looked back over his shoulder and shot him a look. "I already have. Fuck this shit. If this room wants to give us a winning scratch card in exchange for a piece of rubbish like Diane, I say it's a pretty good deal. Just so long as my kids are safe."

To my surprise, Quick hadn't moved from the top of the stairs. He was watching everything in silence. A sadness seemed to have come upon him, his leathery face drooping. I turned and waited for him to do something, but he didn't act. Gradually, I realised it was because it was too late for him to do anything. I turned back to the room, to where Diane was now getting to her feet. Once she was upright, she stared at my mum in astonishment. The thin skin on her elbows had torn away and she was bleeding.

Then a rat appeared at her feet. It was the last thing I

had expected to see. Then several more appeared. Diane noticed them, too, and she began a sort of dance, stepping back and forth to avoid them. She took a step to exit the room but was blocked by a fat rodent the size of a small cat. It pounced on her, grabbing hold of her bleeding elbow and hanging on with its sharp incisors. It swung back and forth as Diane flailed her arms and panicked. Then a second rat pounced and latched onto her thigh, thrashing with its claws and angling its head. It came free, not because it had let go, but because the flesh had come away from Diane's leg. She tried to walk, but the rats multiplied and weaved between her feet, tripping her up, and she fell to the ground. As soon as she was down, a skinny brown beast flew at her face. I covered my mouth in horror as its fangs clamped down on her eyeball and yanked it free. It hung from her cheek like a burst plum.

"Enough!" Quick shouted. "You have this woman, Djall, so take her and be done with it. There is no need to toy with her."

As if the rats understood English, Diane's body disappeared beneath a seething mass of brown and black fur. She didn't so much scream as gargle, and the sound didn't last very long. Three seconds later the door slammed shut. The sudden *clonk* made me scream.

Dad grabbed me and pulled me to his chest. He stank of sweat, but I didn't recoil. Right now, he was the only person I trusted. "Dad, why did Mum do that?"

He didn't answer me.

Sarah stirred nearby, where she was lying, managing to lift her head. Her nose had stopped bleeding and the blister had gone from her face. Colour returned to her cheeks. For a moment she was confused, but then she looked at me. "Martin, is it over?"

Quick glared at my mum and shook his head. "This will never be over for you folks now. There's no going back to the family you once were. No way to forget what happened tonight."

Mum ignored the judgement and rushed over to Sarah, scooped my sister into her arms and squeezed her tightly.

21

Whaen the door on our landing opened again, the room was empty, just an unlit space that shouldn't have been there. Diane's body was nowhere to be seen. Nor was there any blood or rats. Djall had fed and gone away.

Mum had managed to get Sarah to her feet, keeping her trapped in a hug. Dad didn't join them; he remained by me. Both of us shook our heads in silence.

"Something went wrong," said Quick, "and I think I know what it is."

I looked at him. "What?"

He tossed my sister's green glass necklace to the ground and kicked it away. "This isn't Djall's totem. It must be something else. Did you bring anything else into your home that day, from the car boot?"

My mouth was moving before my brain even realised. "Yes, I found something too. It was... Just wait here."

I rushed into my room, which was now a strange, cold place in a house that no longer felt like home. All the same, I knew exactly where to look. I grabbed the Karazy Klown doll from beside my TV and brought it back out onto the landing.

"What's that you have?" Quick asked.

"It's the thing I brought home with me that day. We paid a pound, which was a steal. Maybe the owner wanted rid of it. Could it be Djall's totem?"

The door at the end of the landing slammed and made us flinch. Quick shrugged. "I've known Djall to take the form of dolls before. Not one quite so bizarre-looking, but that's the whole point. Djall takes whatever form it needs for you to covet it."

"If that means I wanted it really bad, then that sounds about right."

Quick snapped his fingers. "Okay, give it to me."

I was about to hand it over when there was a knock at the door. A knock at our *front* door.

Quick turned away from me. "Damn it. We can't afford any more distractions. Who is it?"

"I have no idea."

"I'll make them go away," said Dad, and he hurried downstairs.

The shouting began only a few seconds after I heard the front door open.

Quick looked at me, as uncertain as I had yet seen him. "This keeps getting worse. Give me that doll and I'll get started."

More shouting downstairs. A fight breaking out.

"My dad needs help. We need to go see what's happening down there."

I didn't say so, but I thought I recognised the voice of whoever was arguing with my dad. It filled me with dread.

Quick grabbed me. "Just give me the doll, boy."

I pulled free and started for the stairs, the Karazy Klown

still in my arms. "No, we need to go downstairs and help my dad."

For the first time, Quick seemed angry. I feared him, and thought about how dangerous he could be, but his scowl was only fleeting. He released a pissed-off hiss. "Fine, we'll deal with our unwelcome visitor first, but then you'll do exactly as I say."

I nodded.

The shouting was still going on downstairs, and I now heard something break. Things were getting physical. I ran downstairs, gladdened when I heard Quick thudding down behind me. When I arrived in the hallway, Dad threw up an arm and waved me away. "Stay back, Martin."

"Dad!"

He was fighting with my father – my biological father, Keith – and it looked like he'd been hit. His left eyebrow was fat and puffy. In front of him, Keith shoved and shouldered to try and get to the stairs, but when he saw me he smiled and backed off. "Kiddo! I popped by to see you and Sarah."

There was something wrong with Keith. His face was sweaty and his eyes seemed too big. I didn't want him anywhere near me. "It's late. You shouldn't be here."

"I wanted to see my boy. Hey, where's Sarah? I want to see her too. I bet she's a grown woman now."

Dad placed a hand against Keith's chest and eased him back towards the front door. "It's time to leave."

Keith batted my dad's hand away. "Don't you touch me, you fucking—"

"Fucking *what*, Keith? Why don't you just say it?"

Keith glared at my dad, his hands bunched into fists by his sides. It looked like he might hit him, but instead he stared over at me again. "Martin, please, I just want to speak with you. I was pushed out by this bastard. You've had your head filled with lies. You and Sarah both."

Dad was breathing heavily, and his own hands were now bunched into fists. He barely moved, and yet I had never seen him so angry. "Keith, you need to get out of my house, right now."

Keith sneered. "*Your* house? Thief, that's what you are. You made your bed in my home, you animal."

"There's only one animal here, Keith, and it's not me. You've been drinking, and we both know what that leads to."

"Yeah, me kicking the shit out of you."

Quick moved me aside and stepped up, standing shoulder to shoulder with my dad and facing down Keith. "I think it's time for you to vacate the premises. You're not welcome and it's a bad time."

"Who the hell are you?"

"Thomas Quick... a pleasure. Now leave before I facilitate you doing so."

"I beg you to try it." Keith threw out both hands to shove Quick, but Quick moved like lightning. He stepped aside, creating less of a target, and grabbed his attacker by the wrist. Then, like one of the colourful Spanish matadors I'd seen on TV, he sent my biological father careening past and tumbling under his own weight.

Keith crashed, shoulder-first, into our radiator, then bounced off it and landed amongst our collection of animal statues. One of our giraffes got its neck broken, and the stone elephant tipped onto its side. I gasped, still apparently able to be shocked by violence.

"Don't make me ask again," said Quick.

But Keith didn't look like he was done. He clambered off the floor, growling, and set his sights on Quick. Quick didn't change his posture or even seem concerned in any way. He just stood there, waiting.

"Who the hell are you? You Sharon's new man? Is old Charlie here getting the elbow like I did?"

"I could not be less interested in your story," said Quick, "but unless you leave now, it may end abruptly."

"Yeah, let's see about that."

Keith moved towards Quick, but Mum and Sarah appeared halfway down the stairs and interrupted the scene. Mum no longer seemed dazed; she seemed crazy. Her eyes were fixed wide and she was barely blinking, but when she saw Keith, she bared her teeth. "Get the hell out of here," she spat. "We never want to see you again."

Keith didn't seem to hear her. His eyes were fixed on my sister. "Sarah," he said. "Look at you! You're a picture of your grandmother. It's been too long."

Sarah was stronger than she had been, but she still had to grip the bannister as she came down the stairs. "Dad?"

"Yes, darling, it's me. I'm so sorry that I've been away."

I expected Sarah to be even more confused than I had been when Keith suddenly turned up. I even expected her to be angry. Instead, she leapt off the bottom step and rushed into his outstretched arms. "I missed you," she said, and it hurt me to hear that. It felt like a betrayal.

Keith hugged her tightly, a satisfied grin on his face. Then he moved her back so he could look at her. "Sarah, you're covered in blood. What on earth is going on?"

Sarah broke down in tears. "Dad, it's been so horrible... everything that's happened."

Keith glared at Mum. "Sharon, what have you done to my daughter?"

"Get the fuck out of here, Keith. This doesn't concern you."

"Like hell it doesn't. To think I've been waiting next door, hoping you would come round and we could actually talk. It's clear that I need to get my kids out of this house right now. I should've known you and this pig wouldn't be able to raise them right."

Mum lunged at Keith with her claws outstretched like a cat. Dad had to grab her and hold her, even as she spat and swung her fists.

"We don't have time for this," said Quick. "This is not useful."

Keith focused on Sarah, holding her by the arms and looking into her eyes. "Tell me what happened to you, my love. Where's Diane? She came round to get your mum for me."

Sarah's bottom lip quivered. I prayed she wouldn't speak, but my prayers went unanswered. "I was sick," she said. "Really sick. I think I saw Diane upstairs, but I might have imagined it. Dad, if she went up there then she's dead. They're all dead. It's the room upstairs."

Keith's face fell and the colour drained from his cheeks. Without a word, he moved my sister out of his way and stepped towards the stairs. Quick blocked him immediately but was surprised when my mum threw herself into him. "No," she yelled. "Let the bastard go. Let him see what happened to Diane."

"Sharon, no! Not again." Dad reached out to stop Keith, but Keith struck him with a vicious headbutt that made him cry out and tumble to the floor.

Quick struggled to throw off my mum, but he clearly didn't want to hurt her. She clung on for dear life, keeping him from intervening. All he could do was call out to Keith. "Do not go up there. I'm warning you."

"Fuck you." Keith started up the stairs. "Diane, are you up there? Diane?"

Sarah seemed to realise what was happening. She took a step backwards towards the front door. "Dad, I want to leave. Can we please just leave?"

"Just wait there, my love. I'll take care of this."

I realised I was the only one in any position to do anything, so I raced up the stairs behind Keith, begging him to come back down. He ignored me.

We reached the landing.

The door at the end of the landing was closed. Despite not having set foot in our house for years, Keith noticed it immediately. "There was never a room there before. What is this? How did it get here?"

"Don't open that door, Keith."

He whirled on me, anger in his eyes. "I'm your goddamn father. You don't call me by my name."

"Just... please, don't open that door. Don't even go near it."

"What have they got you involved in, Martin?" He strode towards the door, and I knew he wasn't going to listen to me, so I did the only thing I could – I tackled him. He was twice my size, but I surprised him enough to knock him down to one knee. I threw my weight on top of him and tried to get him down lower, but something struck my face and turned my vision sideways. I fell through a short black tunnel and found myself staring up at the ceiling. Keith had struck me with the back of his hand. Blood filled my mouth.

Keith appeared shocked by his own actions. His eyes opened wide and he shook his head. "I... I'm sorry, but you shouldn't have come at me like that. I'm your father."

I wiped the blood from my mouth, and my head filled

with images of my mum doing the same. Keith was a violent drunk – had always been one.

There was noise from the stairs, and I turned to see my dad climbing onto the landing. He looked at me, likely saw the blood, and his face contorted in horror. The words that came out of his mouth as he glared at Keith were like furious wasps. "I'll kill you, you son of a bitch."

I'd never seen my dad hit anyone before, but he didn't hesitate. He threw a punch with everything he had, and if he'd struck the wall I think the house would have fallen down. Keith ducked the massive haymaker and threw himself forward and lifted my dad up, slamming him against the opposite wall, and part of my dad left a dent in the plasterboard.

Keith followed up his tackle with a punch that hit my dad in the ribs. The sound it made was sickening. I tried to get up and help, but my vision blurred and I tumbled back down. Forced to lie on the ground, I watched while Keith threw another punch and knocked my dad down onto his back.

"You fucking want some, do ya, you black bastard? Take my wife. Take my house. Think you can raise my fucking children?" He went to punch my dad again but doubled over when my dad managed to throw a punch back and hit him in the guts.

"You're the one who left," Dad shouted. "I never tried to replace you. You could have stuck around and been a father, even if you were a shitty husband."

Keith shook off the blow and kneed my dad right in the side of the head as he tried to get up. I saw his eyes glaze over like the wrestlers on TV and I knew the fight had left him. He toppled onto his side and Keith glared down at him. "You took my goddamn wife."

"I couldn't wait to get away," said Mum as she appeared on the landing. Sarah and Quick were right beside her. I don't know if any of them had noticed, but the door at the end of the hallway was slowly opening.

Mercifully, Keith left my dad moaning on the floor and went over to Mum. "You and I were never supposed to end up this way, Sharon. We were good, weren't we? I didn't just come back for the kids, you know? We could be a family again." He looked down at my dad and sneered. "A proper family."

"Just go," said Sarah pleadingly. "Dad, I don't want this. I don't want anyone else to get hurt. I'm sorry for worrying you, but everything is fine."

Keith reached out to hold her, but she flinched. He pulled his hand back slowly and sighed. "Okay, I'll go. Just as soon as I know what happened to Diane. She was trying to help, Sharon. We could have spoken next door like adults."

"I want nothing to do with you. You can die in a ditch for all I care." She moved from between Quick and Sarah and pointed right in his face. "You think I'll ever go back to the beatings and the abuse? You must be insane. I hoped to never see you again. What rock did you climb back from under all of a sudden, anyway?"

"I wished for him to come," I said, realising at once that it was the reason he was here. "I wished for Keith to be here. I'm sorry."

Mum seemed to find it funny, and she shook her head at Keith like he amused her somehow. "I bet you hadn't even given us a second thought until recently, huh? The only reason you're here is because my son made a wish, not because you suddenly realised your responsibilities. You're the same horrible little bully you've always been."

Keith lashed out, grabbing my mother by the hair in the same way she had grabbed Diane less than an hour ago. "You worthless bitch. I should beat that mouth of yours shut."

Quick snatched Keith's hand and glared. "Not a good idea."

Despite the warning, Keith didn't let go of my mum. In fact, he yanked her hair harder and made her cry out. I couldn't bear to watch any longer. I leapt off the ground and tackled him again, just like before. This time, however, I was able to throw him against the wall and pummel him with my fists. He was still too strong for me, though, and it didn't take much for him to toss me back to the ground. I was sure he was going to hit me, but Dad got back on his feet and grabbed Keith before he had the chance. By this time, Keith was a snorting bull, and he struck out with another head-butt, following it up by kicking Dad in the knee. Dad screeched and buckled, grabbing at the wall to keep from falling, but then Keith shoved him so hard that he almost did a cartwheel.

He fell towards the open door at the end of the landing.

I cried out. "No!"

The blackness inside the room reached out for Dad, inky tendrils seeking his flesh. Trying to drag him into hell. Or something like it.

Dad scrambled away, narrowly avoiding the danger at his back. But he couldn't escape the monster in front of him. Keith loomed over him.

From the floor, I looked imploringly at Quick, but he had his hands full trying to keep my mum restrained.

Keith realised the door to the room was open, and he peered into the darkness. "What is this? Is this where you put Diane? What secrets are you hiding? Cannabis? Dodgy videos?"

Dad grabbed at Keith's leg. "Don't!"

"Let him go inside," Mum shouted.

"Quiet, girl," said Quick.

Dad shook his head, blood dripping from his mouth and nose. When he spoke, it sounded like he had a cold. "Sharon, no. Sharon, don't do this."

Keith shut him up with a kick to the side of the head. "Shut your fucking gob! Whatever shit you've got my family into, it ends now."

Dad reached out feebly, trying to keep Keith from going into the room. "Don't..."

Keith kicked him again, this time in the ribs, and then a second time square in the back. Then Keith lost it completely. If I thought he was an animal before, I was certain of it now. He kicked and punched my dad again and again and again, even after he had fallen unconscious. I didn't think he was ever going to stop. Dad was going to end up dead.

I scrambled to my feet, but I was thrown against the wall as someone barged past me. I assumed it was Quick, but it wasn't.

"Get off my dad!" Sarah launched herself at Keith, who looked up in surprise. He was able to react quickly enough to grab her and wrap his arms around her, but the fact he was in the middle of kicking my dad meant he was off balance. Keith tumbled through the open door and fell onto his side. Perhaps instinctively, or maybe out of spite, he kept a hold of Sarah and dragged her inside the room with him, she crashed down on the ground beside him.

"Sarah!" Mum broke free of Quick's large hands and raced towards the room, but the door slammed shut so forcefully that a blast of hot air shot through our landing and knocked us all back. I struck my head on the skirting board as I fell, biting my lip and adding more blood to my mouth. Hands grabbed me and I looked up to see Quick.

"You all right, boy?"

"I-I think so. What just happened?"

Quick didn't answer the question. In fact, he failed to meet my gaze completely as he yanked me to my feet. I looked towards the door. It was open again, but all that lay inside was darkness.

Keith was gone.

Sarah was gone.

Djall had been fed once again.

22

M um erupted into screams. Dad tried to calm her, but she was like a skipping CD, playing the same note over and over again – and there was no way to turn her off.

Through all this, I had somehow kept hold of the Karazy Klown. Now Quick tore it from my hands. "No more delay, boy. The more time we waste, the more people we lose."

I already thought it was too late.

Quick strode across the landing until he was standing before the open room. The darkness crackled and hissed, warning him to stay back. But Quick would not be intimidated. He held up the Karazy Klown and shook it. "Djall! I speak your name and hold your totem. I command you to obey. I command you to release your grip on this family. Return to dormancy at once. This, you cannot refuse."

Nothing happened, and once again I wondered how simple words could affect something so monstrous. Was Quick deluded? Or did he truly know what he was doing? It was too late not to trust him now.

He shook the doll once again, this time more forcefully. "Djall! Leave this place."

The door slammed shut. Opened again. Slammed shut.

"It's not working," I shouted over the din. "Just like before."

Quick ground his teeth, gold glinting. "I don't understand this. Djall, I know you. How do you disobey me?"

I realised this scarred warrior was losing the battle to save our family – what was left of our family – and my gut filled with molten fear. I clasped my sweaty hands together and winced as I felt pain. I studied my hand, seeking the source, and saw that my thumb was red and swollen. The wooden splinter still nestled beneath my flesh. An enemy buried beneath my skin.

I lost my breath.

The jackal.

"You still have the wrong totem," I said, almost laughing at the absurdity of my own words, and at the short sightedness of not having realised it sooner. "It's not my doll."

Quick looked down at the ugly Klown in his hands and hissed. "I'm getting tired of this, boy. What are you talking about?"

"Just wait here. Look after my mum and dad."

Quick nodded, and I took it as his permission to leave. I raced across the landing and jumped down the stairs. I felt a chill at the bottom and took it as a sign. This was the thing we'd been missing, the evil thing hiding in plain sight.

I reached the animal collection beneath our stairs and panicked, for I couldn't see the jackal. Keith had scattered the statues all over the floor when he'd fallen on them, but I could still see the elephant, the giraffes, and all the other creatures. The jackal wasn't there.

Had it changed shape?

Had Djall hidden it to keep us from controlling it?

I sunk to my knees painfully, searching amongst the animals and scattering them even further with my hands. The jackal was not amongst them.

"No, no!" I grabbed my hair and pulled, slumping to the ground as I pictured an imminent future where Djall devoured my parents while I watched. Then it would have me. I was so weak, so battered and bruised, that it was an impossible battle to keep myself upright, and my body ended up flat on the floor. I blinked tears from my eyes and stared into space, trying to take my mind away to some place safe – away from this nightmare that wouldn't end. But there was no escape. All I could do was sob and stare uselessly.

The jackal stared back at me.

It stood upright on all fours beneath the radiator. It must have skittered there after Keith had tumbled. I still couldn't believe he was gone. Truly, I had wanted to get to know him, but now all I was left with were memories of an angry, violent man. What horrors must my mum have endured?

I finally understood why she hated him. Because I hated him too.

The time for thinking wasn't now, so I grabbed the small wooden figurine and scrambled to my feet. I finally had what Quick needed, I just needed to get it to him, but at the foot of the stairs, I fell. My stomach twisted as the worst pain I had ever felt in my life took hold. It folded my body inwards, forcing my knees up to my chest. Every muscle seized. Then I threw up, a vile ocean spilling out from between my lips. I waited for it to pass, but it didn't. My body convulsed again and again. My throat was full and I struggled to breathe. I tried to get up but it was impossible.

Upstairs, my mum continued screaming.

I heard Djall, the door slamming over and over again in a mixture of mockery and hate.

My vision began to curl inwards, growing dark at the edges. I hadn't taken a full breath in almost a minute.

I wondered how long I had before I would be dead.

23

"Martin? Martin, what's wrong?"

My vision existed only as a pinprick, which was why I sensed as much as saw my dad. His hands slid under my body and I felt myself lifted. "Dad?"

"We need to get you to a doctor, Martin. This has gone too far. Quick doesn't know what he's doing. Sarah's gone. She's gone."

"No!" I was weak, but I managed to yell out that one word. Those that followed arrived more quietly. "The jackal. Give him the... the..." I felt another wave of sickness arriving.

"No, Martin, we need to get to the hospital. We need to call the police. Your sister... Your mother."

"Mum? I can still hear her screaming." I felt a draught and I knew my dad was moving towards the front door. "Dad, stop. Is Mum okay?"

"I left her with Quick," he told me. "He was the only one strong enough to keep her from hurting herself. She's in a bad way, which is another reason we need to get help."

"The jackal. Dad, give Quick the jackal before it's too late."

I convulsed in his arms, releasing another wave of vomit. I didn't see where it went, but I didn't hear the sound of it hitting the ground. I felt damp spread through my clothing.

"Are you talking about the jackal I bought from the car boot?"

I puked again, and Dad adjusted his grip on me so that he was holding me like a baby. He stood still and held me until I could speak again. "Y-Yes! The jackal. That's what started all of this. It's Djall's totem."

"I need to get you out of here, Martin. You're my son and I need to keep you safe."

"Dad, please..."

There was silence while Dad stood there with me in his arms. I knew he was thinking. "Okay, fine. Where's the jackal."

I clenched both hands and realised I no longer held it. "The floor. I must have... I must have dropped it."

"I'm going to put you down, okay?"

I murmured that it was okay, and I felt the wooden floor rise up to meet my feet. I reached out and grabbed the bannister to keep from falling. I could still hear my mum screaming. It must have been ten minutes now since she'd started. I feared she might never stop.

I listened to Dad searching until he made a triumphant grunt. "I've got it. Okay, I've got it."

"Dad, go. Give it to Quick."

I heard him race up the stairs, and I sighed with relief. My stomach continued cramping, and yet I couldn't give in to my misery. Clenching my mouth shut, I climbed the first step followed by the next. I started to vomit, no doubt leaving a sickly trail behind me like a slug, but I needed to reach the landing. I needed to know Djall was gone.

Each step was agony, and I had to fight my own traitorous body for every inch. My vision was still a tiny window in a sea of darkness, and every half-breath I struggled to take made that window even smaller. If I passed out, I knew I might never wake again. I remained conscious through willpower alone.

I heard voices in between Mum's screaming. It was my dad talking with Quick. The jackal had to be the totem. If it wasn't...

It had to be. There was nothing else it could be.

I carried on crawling up the stairs, each step a marathon. I feared reaching the top and finding that my family were gone, and in that way my mum's screaming was a comfort. It meant she was still alive.

I finally reached the landing. Dad was holding Mum on the ground, not roughly but firmly enough to keep her thrashing under control. Quick saw me slumped on the steps and came to help me. The small wooden jackal peeked out from his closed fist. "Glad you're not going to miss this, boy. You're sure this is the totem? Third time's the charm, right?"

"Yeah, I'm sure. It has to—" I groaned in pain, my energy spent now that I had completed my journey. Quick dragged me off the steps and sat me up against the wall. With the last of my vision, I watched the room. The door was open, and inside, the darkness swirled and formed an image – a face more serpentine than human. A thing with orb-like eyes full of malice, hunger, and hate. Djall's true face. My blood turned icy in my veins.

Quick stepped in front of me and blocked my view. He held up the wooden jackal. "Djall! I have your totem" – he turned back to me with a grimace – "this time, I'm pretty certain, and I command you to relinquish your hold on this family and this place. Remove your hooks and act no more. I command it. I compel you. You must obey."

A howling wind assaulted the landing, and the door at the end of the landing began slamming shut over and over again, gathering speed. I leaned sideways to get a better view, and each time it opened, I saw that reptilian face glaring back at me. I felt Djall's tendrils in my stomach, squeezing me from the inside, making me want to vomit. I looked at my hands and saw blisters. Quick finally had power over Djall, but before it went it wanted to take a parting shot by killing me. I clutched my sides and groaned.

Quick glanced back at me and appeared nervous. He spoke faster, more forcefully, as he thrust the jackal above his head again. "Djall, I order you to leave this home. Release this family at once. You cannot disobey me, for I have your totem. Obey me! Obey me!"

The door started slamming so rapidly that the banging sound became an endless drone. Our landing transformed into a wind tunnel. The walls began to bleed.

My vision halved, corrupting at the edges. I slid down the wall, almost on my back now. I kept my eyes focused on the door – on Djall's vile face.

"Be gone!" Quick yelled. "Resist me no longer. Your influence is at an end. You will return to solitude. Leave now! I compel you. Remove yourself this very sec—"

There was a high-pitched screech and an explosion of light that made all else disappear. It was so bright that I was glad when the last of my vision went and I plummeted into unconsciousness. Darkness swallowed me.

24

There were police at my home when I woke up, milling about like they owned the place. Several neighbours had apparently reported a disturbance. Among the officers was PC Dorrens, who stood in front of me as I lay on the living room sofa. At first, I wasn't sure why I was alone with him, but then I heard Dad in the hallway trying to get through to Mum, who was talking gibberish. I didn't know where Quick was.

"Martin, are you okay?"

I felt myself, seeking out pain. "I-I think so. What happened?"

Dorrens shook his head, bemused. "The question I've been asking for days. Your family is involved in something, and I'm not going to walk away until I find out what. That can wait though. There's an ambulance on the way to check on you and your family. It looks like someone beat seven shades out of your dad. Would you like to tell me who?"

I stared at him.

"Okay, fine. Then how about you tell me why your mother is clearly in shock? And where's Sarah?"

I could answer none of his questions, but his stare seemed to burn into my skin, a laser beam slowly heating me up. How long before I spilled the madness of what had happened?

Quick entered the room, a mobile phone in his hand like he had just finished a call. I had seen a few mobile phones in the last year – a couple of kids at school even had them – but the one Quick held was half the size of those. He saw PC Dorrens standing over me and frowned. "I'm afraid I'm going to have to ask you not to question the boy without his parents, officer."

Dorrens sighed, but nodded. "Fair enough. Who, might I ask, are you?"

Quick produced an open wallet from his jeans pocket. "Detective Inspector Matthews, Special Branch. Mr Ademale and his family have been helping me with a very sensitive operation. I'm afraid there will be very little they are permitted to tell you."

"I don't believe you. Something is going on here, and I don't know you from Adam. You certainly don't look like you're with Special Branch."

Quick flashed his gold teeth and grinned. "We're an odd bunch, for sure. You may not believe me, but in about thirty seconds, you're going to get a call from your boss asking you to step away immediately. You might think something is going on here, Officer Dorrens, but the truth is above your pay grade. Leave it to the big boys, okay?"

Dorrens' face grew red. He took a step towards Quick and pointed a finger. "You just look here. I'm going to find out exactly what—"

The radio on his shoulder hissed. *Officer Dorrens, please respond.*

Dorrens stared at Quick for several seconds, frozen in

place. Slowly, he broke free and squeezed his radio. "Officer Dorrens responding. Over."

Please return to station. Over.

"What? I'm at a crime scene."

No crime scene. Please return immediately. Over.

Dorrens glared at Quick, but a look of confusion crept onto his face. "This is... wrong."

Please repeat. Over.

"Never mind. PC Dorrens returning to station. Over."

Roger.

Dorrens shook his head at us, looking as disgusted with me as he was with Quick. "This is wrong," he said again, and then he stormed out of the room.

Once the officer was gone, I looked at Quick. "You're a police officer?"

"I can be many things when I want to be, Martin. Whatever gets me the result I need." He sat down on the arm of the sofa, looking down at me. "Now, listen to me, okay? There are going to be people asking questions about what happened here. There're too many missing people for us to stuff the whole thing beneath a rock, but that's okay. I'll protect your family, just so long as you say nothing. Do not speak of these events. A spokesperson will be provided and he or she will say whatever needs to be said. Eventually the questions will stop and you can all go back to living a normal life."

I shook my head. "Sarah's gone. Will she ever be back?"

Quick sighed. He reached down and squeezed my ankle. "I'm sorry, Martin."

"Then there's no normal life to go back to."

"Perhaps I misspoke. All the same, life is not over for you. You're a brave lad, and this world favours the brave. I'll be checking in on you, and if there's anything you need..."

He looked towards the hall, to where my parents were huddled in a broken mess. "If there's anything any of you need, I'll be there."

"My mum needs help."

Quick nodded.

"Is Djall gone?"

Quick held up a small see-through plastic case. The wooden jackal rattled about inside. "Not gone, but contained. Unfortunately, the Sphere knows no way to destroy Djall for good, but he'll be under lock and key until the end of time if I have anything to say about it. I'm sorry this happened to you, Martin. Truly. The man who betrayed our order... He was my best friend. It was *my* trust he took advantage of in order to steal from the vaults. I failed at my duty, and your family has paid for it. I wish I could say the guilt will keep me awake at night, but honestly, it'll just get lost amongst the lifetime's worth I already have."

"I forgive you," I said.

Quick's eyes widened. "You forgive me? Just like that?"

I nodded. "It's not your fault evil things exist, but I feel better knowing there are people like you trying to fight it. I think you have it wrong though. I think the Sphere is wrong."

"How so?"

"You keep the monsters hidden, trying to fight them in secret. How can that be right?"

"It keeps society from spiralling into chaos."

"No... If everyone knew about things like Djall, then we could all fight together. We could all make life harder for the monsters. Now that I know, I won't be scared next time. I'll just fight."

"Next time? Martin, I sincerely hope there will never be a next time for you. I understand the wisdom of what you're saying, and perhaps the Sphere does have it wrong, but that's something far, far above my station." He squeezed my ankle again. "I have some more calls to make. You going to be okay for a little while?"

I nodded.

"Good." Quick got up and turned towards the door. He was about to leave but then turned back and tutted. "I almost forgot. I found this on the ground. Make sure your dad makes use of it."

I took the scratch card he handed to me and frowned. "Huh? This was because of Djall. Get it away from me!"

"No, boy, it's a hundred grand. Cash it in. Give your poor family some breathing room."

"It's cursed. If we cash it in then bad things will happen."

Quick shook his head. "Djall grants wishes, and if you wished for a hundred grand then that scratch card is as real as you and I. Use it."

"But there'll be a debt to pay."

"All debts are void. When I broke Djall's hold on you, he lost all power over your family. You're safe. Get your money and don't look back. It's the least you deserve."

Quick left the room, leaving me holding the scratch card. I thought about what a hundred grand could do for my family, but none of it seemed to matter without Sarah.

I would never see my sister again.

We couldn't even bury her.

All at once, my body turned inside out and I began to sob uncontrollably, weeping so deeply that I could barely breathe. A few minutes later, I heard my mum and dad do exactly the same.

It went on for weeks.

And then months.

25

"And so you see," I said as I looked down at my notes sitting atop of the dais, "the evil that entered my home that pleasant Sunday after the car boot was not a temporary blight on my family. Its corruption was permanent. My sister had her life cut short before her sixteenth birthday, and my mother never recovered. We tried to help her with drugs and therapy – and expensive holidays with the scratch card money – but eventually she had to be committed. She died four years ago, barely knowing who I was. My dad died nine years ago, a man who no longer smiled. He raised me to adulthood but then seemed to give up on life. Djall took a piece of us all that would never heal. It was only me who managed to use what happened in a positive way. For, you see, I meant what I said that day to Caretaker Quick. If mankind knew about the monsters under its bed, people would stop being prey and start being hunters. There is no strength in hiding the threats to our world. In a war, the side with the most soldiers wins, and for far too long we have been outnumbered. That is why you are all here."

I looked out at the assembly hall, taking in the faces of all three hundred new recruits – young men and women with bright minds and brave spirits. Some had encountered evil in the same way I had, but others had been headhunted and then initiated. We were letting the cat halfway out of the bag by swelling our ranks, but soon we would have abominations like Djall on the run. Soon, there would be no more devastated families like mine. The world would be a safer place for all.

When Quick had said he would be there for me, that he would provide whatever I needed, the only thing I could think of was an escape. A new life.

As soon as I finished school, I had contacted him. Then I had demanded a job. If I hadn't joined the Sphere then I would have grown into an angry, broken man. I needed a purpose, some way to use the pain inside me for good. Being able to fight back against things like Djall was that purpose.

I rose to the station of caretaker younger than anyone had in over a hundred years, and within a decade I was the youngest cohort leader in the country. Now I was legate in charge of recruitment, a post created especially for me after I had pushed for so long to add more members to our organisation. The Sphere was where I belonged, and I peered towards the back of the room to offer a nod of gratitude to the man who had been there at my side for almost twenty years. Thomas Quick didn't look any older than the day I met him in the hospital, but he had added more scars to his collection. He had taken to wearing gloves to hide his battered hands, and he had exchanged his leather jacket for a high-collared woollen one. It was 2019.

"All of you are about to embark on a lifelong career," I said to my new recruits. "There is no going back from here, no unlearning the things you will learn, no unseeing the things you will see, but take heart that your life will be dedicated to the forces of good. For every person you fail, you will save the lives of three more. We are winning this war, and you are going to help tip the scales even further. Each one of you is a warrior, a hero, a soldier. Each of you is a stranger in the night, saving the weak and helping the helpless. Soon, you will be caretakers of the world's worst evils. It should be a lonely job, a frightening job, but it is anything but. We are family. Your brothers and sisters will face the darkness with you, and you will never be alone again. I welcome you all to the Sphere of Zosimus."

The audience erupted in applause. They always did. This was my third batch of new recruits – my first included an ageing yet determined police officer named Dorrens – and other countries were starting to adopt our methods too. It warmed my heart to feel my family growing.

I stepped down from the dais, excited about the days to come, for I was Martin Gable, caretaker of evil.

WANT FREE BOOKS?

Don't miss out on your FREE Iain Rob Wright horror pack. Five bestselling horror novels sent straight to your inbox at no cost. No strings attached & signing up is a doddle.

Just visit www.iainrobwright.com

PLEA FROM THE AUTHOR

Hey, Reader. So you got to the end of my book. I hope that means you enjoyed it. Whether or not you did, I would just like to thank you for giving me your valuable time to try and entertain you. I am truly blessed to have such a fulfilling job, but I only have that job because of people like you; people kind enough to give my books a chance and spend their hard-earned money buying them. For that I am eternally grateful.

If you would like to find out more about my other books then please visit my website for full details. You can find it at:

www.iainbwright.com.

Also feel free to contact me on Facebook, Twitter, or email (all details on the website), as I would love to hear from you.

If you enjoyed this book and would like to help, then you could think about leaving a review on Amazon, Goodreads, or anywhere else that readers visit. The most important part of how well a book sells is how many positive reviews it has, so if you leave me one then you are directly helping me to continue on this journey as a full time writer. Thanks in advance to anyone who does. It means a lot.

Iain Rob Wright is one of the UK's most successful horror and suspense writers, with novels including the critically acclaimed, THE FINAL WINTER; the disturbing bestseller, ASBO; and the wicked screamfest, THE HOUSEMATES.

His work is currently being adapted for graphic novels, audio books, and foreign audiences. He is an active member of the Horror Writer Association and a massive animal lover.

www.iainrobwright.com
FEAR ON EVERY PAGE

For more information
www.iainrobwright.com
iain.robert.wright@hotmail.co.uk

Lightning Source UK Ltd.
Milton Keynes UK
UKHW012243050620
364507UK00002B/460